KU-264-815

Alex bit out a curse he hadn't uttered since his college days. "I'm not the right guy for you, Isabel."

She gave him a determined look. "I'm talking about a kiss. Not the rest of our lives. Please answer the question," she pleaded, "otherwise I'm going to feel like a total idiot. Good or bad—I can take it."

He pressed his hands to his temples. It had taken a lot of nerve to ask that question. And it had been *his* mistake in ever admitting he found her attractive. "Yes," he conceded finally. "I want to kiss you. But—"

"Alex." The tension in her face slid away. "Get on with it, will you?"

"This is an insanely bad idea," he groaned.

But he was already stepping into her and lowering his mouth to the lush temptation in front of him. One kiss couldn't hurt—could it?

Jennifer Hayward has been a fan of romance and adventure since filching her sister's Harlequin Mills & Boon® novels to escape her teenaged angst. She penned her first romance at nineteen. When it was rejected, she bristled at her mother's suggestion that she needed more life experience. She went on to complete a journalism degree and to intern as a sports broadcaster before settling into a career in public relations. Years of working alongside powerful, charismatic CEOs and travelling the world provided perfect fodder for the arrogant alpha males she loves to write about, and free research on some of the world's most glamorous locales.

With a suitable amount of life experience under her belt, she sat down and conjured up the sexiest, most delicious Italian wine magnate she could imagine, had him make his biggest mistake and gave him a wife on the run. That story, THE DIVORCE PARTY, won her Harlequin's *So You Think You Can Write* contest and a book contract. Turns out Mother knew best!

With the first item on her bucket list complete, Jennifer is now working her way through the rest. She put Number Two in the bag when she talked her way into the jumpseat of an Airbus for landing on a flight from San José to Toronto, complete with headphones and a flight plan. The only thing missing was a follow-up date with the Robert Redford lookalike pilot. Figuring that Number Three—walking the runway as an angel at the Victoria's Secret Christmas fashion show—is not likely to happen, she's concentrating on Numbers Four and Five, which include touring Australia and building a dream beach house in Barbados.

A native of Canada's gorgeous east coast, Jennifer now lives in Toronto with her Viking husband and their young Viking-in-training. She considers her ten-year-old-strong book club, comprised of some of the most amazing women she's ever met, a sacrosanct date in her calendar. And some day they will have their monthly meeting at her fantasy beach house, with waves lapping at their feet, wine glasses in hand.

You can find Jennifer on Facebook and Twitter.

Recent titles by the same author:
THE TRUTH ABOUT DE CAMPO
AN EXQUISITE CHALLENGE
THE DIVORCE PARTY

Did you know these are also available as eBooks?
Visit www.millsandboon.co.uk

CHANGING CONSTANTINOU'S GAME

BY
JENNIFER HAYWARD

All rights reserved including the right of reproduction in whole
or in part in any form. This edition is published by arrangement with
Harlequin Books S.A.

This is a work of fiction. Names, characters, places, locations and
incidents are purely fictional and bear no relationship to any real
life individuals, living or dead, or to any actual places, business
establishments, locations, events or incidents. Any resemblance is
entirely coincidental.

This book is sold subject to the condition that it shall not, by way of
trade or otherwise, be lent, resold, hired out or otherwise circulated
without the prior consent of the publisher in any form of binding or
cover other than that in which it is published and without a similar
condition including this condition being imposed on the subsequent
purchaser.

® and TM are trademarks owned and used by the trademark owner
and/or its licensee. Trademarks marked with ® are registered with the
United Kingdom Patent Office and/or the Office for Harmonisation in
the Internal Market and in other countries.

Published in Great Britain 2014
by Mills & Boon, an imprint of Harlequin (UK) Limited,
Eton House, 18-24 Paradise Road, Richmond, Surrey, TW9 1SR

© 2014 Jennifer Drogell

ISBN: 978-0-263-24291-1

Harlequin (UK) Limited's policy is to use papers that are natural,
ren............................ .... in
sus .... conform
to 1...................... .... 1.

Pri ....
by

MORAY COUNCIL LIBRARIES & INFO.SERVICES	
20 37 55 56	
Askews & Holts	
RF RF	

CHANGING CONSTANTINOU'S GAME

For the Watermill Writers—
Alison, Helene, Jo, Lesa, Louise, Pippa, Rachael,
Sharon and Suzie. Remembering my week with you all
in Tuscany, listening to stories of rhinestone-studded
cat collars, peach thongs and lines like 'flattered but not
tempted' puts a smile on my face always. I love you all.

And thank you to Mike, the elevator repair technician who
took away some of my drama, and who also educated me
on how very, very safe elevators are! I think I'll take the
less dramatic ride for the rest of my life. :)

CHAPTER ONE

As FAR AS luck went, Manhattan-based reporter Isabel Peters had been enjoying more than her fair share of it lately. She'd managed to nab a cute little one-bedroom on the Upper East Side she could actually afford, she'd won a free membership to the local gym, which might actually enable her to keep off the fifteen pounds she'd recently lost, and because she'd been in the right place at the right time, she'd landed a juicy story about the New York mayoral race that was putting her name on the map at the network.

But as she raced through the doors of Sophoros's London offices, slapped her card down on the mahogany reception desk in front of the immaculately dressed receptionist and blurted out her request to see Leandros Constantinou, the look on the blonde's face suggested her lucky streak might finally have run out.

"I'm afraid you've missed him, Ms. Peters," the receptionist said in that perfectly accented English that never failed to make Izzie feel totally unworthy. "Mr. Constantinou is already on his way back to the States."

Damn. The adrenaline that had been rocketing through her ever since her boss had texted her as she was about to board her flight home from Italy this morning and sent her on a wild-goose chase across London came to a screeching, sputtering halt, piling up inside her like a three-car collision. She'd done everything she could to make it here before Sophoros's billionaire CEO left. But midday traffic hadn't been on her side. Neither had her poky cab driver, who hadn't seemed to recognize the urgency of her mission.

She struggled to control the frustration that was no doubt writing its way across her face, reminding herself that this woman could still be useful. "Thank you," she murmured, wrapping her fingers around the card and sliding it back into her purse. "Would you happen to know which office he's headed for?"

"You would have to ask his PA that," the blonde said with a pointed look. "She's in the New York headquarters. Would you like her number?"

"Thanks, I have it." Izzie chewed on her bottom lip. "How long ago did he leave?"

"Hours," the other woman drawled. "So sorry it was a wasted trip."

Something about the gleam in the gatekeeper's eyes made Izzie give her a second look. Was the elusive Leandros Constantinou holed up in his office avoiding her? She wouldn't put it past him from what her boss had said about his magic disappearing acts when it came to the press, but she didn't have time to flush him out. Her flight back to New York left in exactly three and a half hours, and she intended to be on it.

She gave the other woman a nod, zipped up her purse and turned away from the desk. James, her boss, wasn't going to be happy about this. From what he'd said in his texts, the scandal rocking Constantinou's gaming software company was about to go public. And if NYC-TV didn't get to him before it did and persuade him to do the interview, every media outlet in the country was going to be knocking on his door. At that point, their chances of landing the feature would be slim to none.

She swung her purse over her shoulder with a heavy sigh and made her way out the heavy glass doors to the bank of elevators. A glance at the bored, restless expressions of those in the packed reception area told her she'd walked right into the middle of the midday caffeine and nicotine exodus. Which wasn't to say she herself didn't have bad habits. Hers were just more of the "shoving food she didn't need in her mouth" variety. Or obsessing over a story when she should be at the gym sweating off a few extra pounds. But what was a girl to do when her mother was a famous Hollywood diva and her sister sashayed down runways for a living? Perfection was never going to be all that attainable.

The ping of an elevator arriving pulled her gaze to the row of silver-coated death traps. A group of people crammed themselves inside like a pack of sardines, and she should have gone with them, really, given her hurry. But her heart, which hadn't quite recovered from the trip up, started pounding like a jackhammer. Just looking at the claustrophobic eight-by-eight-foot box made her mouth go dry and her legs turn to mush.

She glanced at the fire exit door, wondering how bad, exactly, walking down fifty flights of stairs would be. *Bad,* she decided. Three-inch heels did not lend themselves to such activity and besides, she *had* to catch that flight. Better to slay her demons and get on with it. Except, she reasoned, taking a step back as the thick steel doors slammed shut on the dozen people inside, having a whole contingent bear witness to her incapacitating fear of elevators wasn't going to happen.

Telling herself she was a rational, levelheaded woman with what many would call a heck of a lot of responsibility on her shoulders every day, she looked desperately around the lobby at the crowd that was left in search of a diversion. She could do this. She wasn't a total head case.

She took in the drop-dead perfect figure of the woman to her right, covered in a body-hugging dress that screamed haute couture. *Stunning. Were these women everywhere?* And weren't those designer heels? *So not fair.* The only pair of designer shoes she owned were a ruby-red marked-down find she'd fallen in love with, then spent a quarter of a month's salary on. Which had seen her eating cereal for dinner for weeks.

She kept her gaze moving. Over a man who looked as if he indulged in one too many pastries at tea every day to the distinctly *not* middle-aged specimen leaning against the wall beside him typing on his smartphone. Her jaw dropped. How could she have missed *him*? He was distraction with a capital *D*. And even that didn't begin to describe the six-foot-something-inches of pure testosterone in the designer suit. He was distraction in all caps. And then some…

Wow. She took in every magnificent inch of him. She'd never seen a guy wear a suit *that* well. Not even the full-of-themselves peacocks who liked to show off in the financial district bars of Manhattan. Because the way the tailored dark gray creation molded this man's tall, lean frame to perfection? Should be illegal. Particularly the way it hugged his muscular, to-die-for thighs like a glove.

Damn but he was hot. Like "her body temperature ratcheted up about ten degrees" hot. She dragged her gaze northward to check out his swarthy, sexy Mediterranean profile. And froze. Somewhere along the way he'd looked up from his phone…*at her.* Lord. That dimple, indentation, or whatever you called it in the middle of his chin—it was just so…*yum.*

She held her breath as he embarked on a perusal that bore little resemblance to her guilty ogling. No—this was a fully adult, ultra-confident assessment of her assets by a man who'd surely had his pick of those he'd bestowed it upon in the past. She twitched, pushing her feet into the floor, wanting to squirm like a six-year-old. But her training as a reporter had taught her that was the last thing she should do when cornered. By the time his gaze moved back to her face, unleashing a full blast of heady dark blue on her, she was sure her cheeks weren't the only thing that were beet-red.

A long moment passed—which surely had to be the most excruciating of her life. Then he broke the contact with a deliberate downward tilt of his chin, his attention moving back to his phone.

Dismissed.

Her cheeks flamed hotter. *Honestly, Izzie, what were you expecting? That he would ogle you back? This has been happening your entire life. With men who weren't that far out of your league.*

A Latin tune filled the air. Grew louder. Adonis lifted his head; frowned. *Her phone. Dammit.* She fumbled in her bag and pulled it out.

"So...?" Her boss barked. "What happened?"

"He was already gone, James, sorry. Traffic was bad."

Her boss let out a short, emphatic expletive. "I'd heard he was uncatchable but I thought that was only for the female population."

Izzie had no idea what Leandros Constantinou looked like—or anything about him for that matter. She'd never heard of the gaming company he ran, nor its wildly popular racing title, *Behemoth*, before this morning when she'd gotten James's text on the way home from her girls' trip to Tuscany and he'd ordered her to make this pit stop. His text had said Constantinou's former head of software development, Frank Messer, who'd been pushed out of the company years ago, had walked into NYC-TV today claiming he was the brains behind *Behemoth*. Determined to get his due, he'd launched a court case against the company.

And offered an exclusive interview to her boss to tell his side of the story.

She pursed her lips. "I asked the receptionist which office he was headed for, but she wouldn't tell me."

"My source says it's New York." Her boss sighed. "No worries, Iz, we'll get him here. He can't avoid us forever."

We? She frowned. "Are you going to let me work on this?"

There was silence on the other end of the line. "So I wasn't going to tell you until you got back, given that you get yourself all worked up about stuff like this, but since the timing's changed I better let you know now. Catherine Willouby is retiring. The network execs have been impressed with your work of late and they want you to try out to replace her."

Her breath caught in her lungs, her stomach doing a loop-to-loop. She took an unsteady step backward. Catherine Willouby, NYC-TV's much-loved matriarch and weekend anchor, was retiring? And they wanted *her*, a lowly community reporter with a handful of years of experience to audition to replace her?

"But I'm two decades younger than her," she sputtered. "Don't they want someone with more experience?" And wasn't she an idiot for even mentioning that fact?

"We're getting killed with the younger demographic," James said flatly. "They think you can bring in some of that age group, plus you already have a great relationship with the community."

Her head spun. She wiped a clammy palm against her skirt. She should be over the moon that they thought that highly of her. But her stomach was too busy tying itself up in knots. "So what does this have to do with the Constantinou story?"

"The execs think your weak spot is a lack of hard news experience…something your competition has tons of. So

I'm going to hand you this story and you're going to knock it out of the park."

Oh. She swallowed hard. Pressed her phone tighter against her ear and rocked back on her heels. The Constantinou story was going to make headlines across the country. *Was she ready for this?*

"You still there?" James demanded.

"Yes," she responded, her voice coming out a high-pitched squeak. She closed her eyes. "Yes," she repeated firmly.

"Stop freaking out," he admonished. "It's an interview—that's all. You might not get any further than that."

An interview in the biggest media market in the world, likely in front of a panel of stiff-suited network execs who would analyze her down to her panty hose brand...

The knot in her stomach grew bigger. "When?"

"Ten a.m. tomorrow, here at the station."

Tomorrow? She shot a glance at an arriving elevator. "James, I—"

"I gotta go, Iz. I've emailed you some prep questions. Rehearse them inside out and you'll be fine. Ten a.m. Don't be late."

The line went dead. She stood there dumbfounded. *What had just happened?*

The tall, dark-haired hunk picked up his bag and moved toward the empty elevator. A quick scan of the lobby told her they were the only two left. She tossed her phone in her purse and made herself follow. Except five feet from the doors, her feet glued to the spot and refused to move. She stood there staring at the empty metal cube, her pulse rate skyrocketing. The hunk pushed his hand courteously against the door as it started to close, impatience playing around the edges of his mouth. "You coming?"

She nodded, momentarily distracted by the New York

accent mixed with the sexy faint flavoring of something foreign. Greek, maybe?

Move, she told herself, managing a couple of tentative steps toward the terrifying little box. But the closer she got, the harder it was to drag oxygen into her constricted lungs. She came to a skittering halt a foot away.

His gaze narrowed on her face. "You okay?"

She inclined her head. "Slight fear of elevators."

His brow furrowed. "Millions of people travel in them every day…they're unbelievably safe."

"It's the unbelievable part I worry about," she muttered, staying where she was.

He rolled his eyes. "How do you get to work every day?"

"I take the stairs."

His mouth tightened. "Look, I have to get to the airport. You can take this one or the next…your choice."

She swallowed. "Me too…have to get to the airport, I mean."

He gave her a steady look, visibly controlling his impatience. "Get on, then."

A vision of her and her sister curled up in a dark elevator yelling for help flashed through her head. Like it always did when she had to make herself do this. She remembered the utter silence of the heavy metal box as they'd sat there shivering against the wall for hours, their knees drawn up to their chins, terrified it was going to drop. Her absolute conviction that nobody was ever going to find them and they were going to spend the night in the cold, silent darkness.

He let out an oath. "I have to go."

She stared at him blankly as he jabbed his finger against the button, his words bouncing off the terror freezing her brain. The heavy metal doors started to close.

She could not miss that flight.

Dragging in a deep breath, she dived forward, shoving her bag between the closing doors, then throwing her body through after it. Adonis cursed, jamming his hand into the opening. "What the hell?" he ground out as she landed against the back of the elevator, palms pressed to the metal to steady herself. "What kind of a stupid maneuver was that?"

She jumped as the doors slammed shut. "I have a job interview tomorrow...I can't miss my flight."

"So you thought that getting there in multiple pieces was a better idea?" He shook his head and looked at her as though she was a crazy person.

"Slight fear of elevators...remember?" She wrapped her fingers around the smooth metal bar that surrounded the elevator and held on for dear life.

He lifted a brow. "Slight fear?"

She nodded, leaning back against the bar in as casual a pose as she could manage with her shaking knees threatening to topple her. "Don't mind me. I'm good."

He didn't look convinced, but transferred his attention to the television screen running a ticker recap of the day's news. A couple of minutes tops, she told herself. Then she'd be back on solid ground and on her way to the airport.

The elevator moved smoothly downward, whizzing through the floors. She started to think she *was* a little crazy. This wasn't so bad... She took a couple of deep, steadying breaths and relaxed her fingers around the bar. She could do this, she repeated like a mantra in her head, glancing up at the numbers as they lit up. Just thirty-four more floors...

A couple of businessmen immersed in a politically incorrect joke joined them on the thirty-third floor, their deep voices booming in the echoing confines of the elevator. By the time they got off on the thirty-second floor,

Izzie was smiling. Perhaps not socially acceptable, but the joke *was* funny.

The elevator picked up speed again. And more speed. She whipped her gaze up to the LCD panel. Thirty-one, thirty, twenty-nine... Was it her imagination, or were the floors whizzing by faster than before? Her heartbeat accelerated. She *must* be imagining it because elevators didn't change speed, did they? The numbers whizzed by faster. She flicked an alarmed look at the hunk. He was staring at the numbers too. Twenty-eight, twenty-seven, twenty-six...*they were definitely accelerating.*

"Wh-what's happening?" she croaked, clutching the bar behind her.

He swung around, his mouth set in a grim line. "I don't—"

The rest of his words were ripped from his mouth as the elevator slammed to a sudden, screeching halt. She shrieked as the force of the impact tore her hands from the bar and sent her careering forward. The stranger lunged for her, but the bouncing elevator threw him off balance and he slammed into her. The floor came up to meet them, the heavy weight of his body crashing down on hers. The sound of her head hitting the tile reverberated in her ears. Then everything went silent.

Alex lay on top of the girl, fighting to pull air into his lungs. The car swayed and creaked — seemed to be making up its mind whether to stay put or not. He froze, not daring to move, until several seconds had passed and the elevator remained where it was. An eerie silence consumed the space. *The emergency brakes must have deployed.* Thank. God.

The sound of frantic, staccato breathing filled his ear. His face was buried in a sea of thick, silky hair, the weight of his body crushing the woman's smaller, slighter frame.

He cursed inwardly, wondering how badly he'd hurt her. In trying to catch her, he'd taken her out hard—like an outside linebacker on a mission.

He pressed his hands against the tile and levered himself gingerly off her. She was lying facedown on the floor, motionless except for her frantic breathing. He curved a hand around her shoulder. "Are you okay?"

She didn't respond, her breath coming in gasping mouthfuls. He slid an arm underneath her and gently turned her over. Her glassy eyes and paper-white face made his heart pound. *Christós.* The nasty purple bump beginning to form on the left side of her forehead made it accelerate even faster.

He trained his gaze on hers until she focused on him. "Are you okay?"

Her lips parted. "The—the elevator... Are w-we stopped?"

He let out a long breath. "Yes. The emergency brakes kicked in."

Relief filled her glazed eyes. But it didn't last long. Her gaze darted, bouncing like a tennis ball off the metal walls, her quick, gasping breaths increasing in speed as her fingers dug into the tile floor and she tried to push herself into a sitting position. "I— I can't—I don't—"

He gripped her shoulders and pushed her back to the floor. "You need to calm down or we're going to be in even more trouble here," he ordered. "Deep breaths, in and out."

She stared at him, chest heaving, eyes huge.

"*Now.*" He slid his fingers under her chin and held her immobile. "Breathe. In and out."

She pulled in a breath. Then another. They were quick, shallow pulls of air, but more than before and gradually, her breathing slowed. "Good," he nodded approvingly. "Keep it up."

He kept her breathing in and out until the panic receded from her eyes and her face regained some color.

"Better?" he asked softly.

"Yes, thank you." She pulled in another deep breath, blinked and looked around. "I can't see...my glasses," she murmured. "I must have lost them in the fall."

He stood and searched for them. Found them in the corner of the elevator, miraculously intact. He carried them back to her, knelt down and slid them on her face. "You hit your head. Are you dizzy at all?"

She sat up slowly. Twisted her head to the left and right. "Not unless I think about the fact that I'm in here."

"Then don't." He stood up and moved toward the control panel. Pulled the phone from behind a metal door and barked a greeting. The line crackled and a young male voice responded. "Everybody okay in there?"

"Yes," Alex said grimly. "Are we stable?"

"Yes, sir. We had an issue with the generator, but the emergency brakes deployed."

His heartbeat slowed, his grip on the receiver relaxing. "How long until you get us out?"

"We're working on getting a crew over there as soon as we can. But by the time we do that and assess how we're going to get you out of there, it may be a few hours."

He flicked a glance at the white-faced woman on the floor. "By that you mean...?"

"The car you're in is stuck between floors. In that situation, we either try to move the car manually from the control room and pry the doors open or we take you out the top. Obviously we'd prefer to do the former, but with the generator out that may not be possible."

He moved his gaze over the bump on the woman's face, the fact that he was going to miss his flight a far lower priority than her potential injuries. "The sooner the better...."

The other passenger in here with me—she hit her head when we stopped."

"We'll go as fast as we can," the technician promised. "Anything else I can do for you?"

"Hurry up," Alex muttered roughly and hung up. Telling the guy he owned half the building wasn't going to make it happen any faster.

The woman watched him with those big brown eyes of hers, her tense expression only this side of full-on panic.

"When are they going to get us out of here?"

He walked back over to her and sank down on his haunches. "They have to get a technician here and see what's happening. It may take a while."

Her gaze sharpened on his face. "Don't they just pry the doors open?"

He hesitated, wondering whether or not to tell her the truth. "We're stuck between floors," he said finally. "A generator's out, which means they can't move us."

Her eyes widened, her hands flailing as she sat up and stared at him. "*What*?"

"Calm down," he ordered. "They'll find a way, but panicking isn't going to help."

Her throat convulsed. "How long did they say?"

"A few hours."

"*I can't be in here that long.*" She fixed her gaze on his. "I really, really don't do elevators."

He took her hands in his. They were clammy and she was shaking like a leaf. "Look—" he said, arching a brow at her. "What's your name?"

"Izzie."

"*Izzie?*"

"Short for Isabel," she elaborated, distractedly. "But most people call me Izzie."

"Isabel," he elected to use instead, his tone firm but reassuring, "I promise you everything's going to be fine.

These guys handle situations like this all the time. They're going to get a crew over here, figure out how to get us out and in a few hours you'll be laughing this off."

She looked at him as though he had two heads.

"Okay," he conceded. "But you know what I mean. It's going to be fine, I promise."

She stared at him for a long moment, her teeth worrying her lip. "You're sure? We aren't going to drop again?"

"I'm sure."

She lifted her chin. "All right. I can do this."

"Good girl."

She pressed her lips together. "Since you're the only thing keeping me sane, you could tell me *your* name."

"Alex." He let go of her hands and pushed to his feet. Located her discarded bag and picked it up. "Anything in here we can use to get the swelling down on your head?"

She shook her head. "I'm not sure."

"Can I look?"

She nodded.

He sat down beside her and riffled through it. The bag was a modern marvel of how much a woman could shove into a few cubic inches of leather. Chocolate, water, books, a brush, a *full bottle of aspirin...*

"Is there anything you *don't* have in here?" he questioned drily. "I'll never understand why you women feel you have to carry half your lives around with you. There is a drugstore on every corner, you know...."

She wrinkled her nose at him. "That's a bit of an exaggeration."

He pulled out a lint brush. "Really? You need to carry a lint brush with you?"

A pink stain filled her cheeks. "Have you ever sat on a cat-infested sofa in a black wool skirt?"

"Can't say that I have," he drawled. "You've got me

on that one." He pulled out a can of still-cold soda. "How about this? It could work."

"Wait," she gasped, sitting up. "My flight takes off in a few hours."

"So does mine," he returned grimly. "I think we can safely assume we're not making it."

"But I have to..." she burst out. "I have that interview in Manhattan tomorrow morning."

"You're going to have to reschedule your flight," he told her, handing her the can of soda. "And hope you can get another tonight."

She sliced a panicked look at her watch. He glanced at his. Two forty-five. There wasn't a hope in hell he was making his flight to New York. Which was a problem; with Frank Messer trying to rip his company apart, he was putting out fires left, right and center, and the Sophoros jet was under maintenance at Heathrow, necessitating a commercial flight.

"Ouch." She winced as she held the can to the now robin's egg-sized lump on her forehead. He leaned over, tipped her chin up with his fingers and inspected the bump. "You're going to be black and blue for a while, but hopefully that's all it'll be."

She stared at him with a deer-in-the-headlights expression that should have warned him off, but didn't. He was far too busy noticing how the lashes on her almond-shaped, exotic eyes were a mile long and how those full lips of hers could take him to the moon and back should she choose to apply them correctly...

And what the hell was he thinking? He let go of her chin and shifted away from her. She was attracted to him. She'd made that clear upstairs in the lobby. And of course he'd noticed her. It had been hard not to. Disheveled, distracted, she'd been jabbering into her mobile phone in a husky, breathless voice that had made it easy to envision her in his bed. That and that body… The kind of curves that would look even better without clothes.

He shook his head and looked in the opposite direction. Not the kind of thinking that boded well for hours in close proximity.

"Alex?"

She was holding out a bottle of water, her cheeks even pinker than before. "Want one?"

He took it, if only to cool down his overheated libido. A paperback spilled out of her bag, a half-dressed woman in the arms of a bare-chested male emblazoned on the cover.

He picked it up. "Do you actually read this stuff?" he demanded incredulously.

"I do," she said stiffly. "Can I please have it back?"

He ignored her outstretched hand. Turned the book over. "Looks smutty…is that why you women like it?"

"I suppose you have *Othello* in your bag," she came back tartly, reaching for it.

He pulled it away. "Actually, *Great Expectations*. Want to have a browse?"

She gave him a long look. "You've got to be kidding."

He braced his hands on the floor to roll to his feet. She waved him off. "Okay, I believe you. You've had your laugh…can I have my book back, please?"

He gave her a considering look. "It *is* smutty, isn't it?"

She glared at him. Watched as he flipped pages, stopped to read one, then moved on. He halted at a particularly juicy section. "Oh this is good." He quoted out loud, deepening his voice to add an over-the-top commentary. "He ran his finger over her erect nipple, making her groan in response…Ellie—" he flicked a glance at her, "who calls their characters Ellie, by the way? Anyway," he looked back at the book, "Ellie arched her back and—"

"*Alex*," she pleaded, dropping the can and lunging for the book. "Give it to me."

He held it away from her. "I just want to know. What's the appeal? That a guy's going to charge in on a white steed and carry you off, and you'll live happily ever after?"

"I don't need a man to rescue me," she muttered, sitting back and wrapping her arms around herself. "I can do my own rescuing."

"That," he stated drily, "is up for debate." He handed the book back to her.

She shoved it in her bag with a decisive movement. He decided to be a humanitarian and move on. "So what are you doing in London? Work or play?"

"I'm doing a favor for my boss." She grimaced and pressed the can tighter to her head. "It was supposed to be a quick in and out on my way home from Italy."

"Just your luck," he grinned. "You picked the one faulty elevator in London."

"Please don't remind me."

"What line of work are you in?"

She took a sip of her water. "Communications… You?"

"I own an entertainment company, based in New York." He leaned back against the wall, keeping up the small talk he abhorred as it seemed to be putting a bit of color back into her cheeks. "Was Italy work too?"

She shook her head. "I was doing a cooking course with my girlfriends in Tuscany. We rented a villa on the coast, chilled out and learned how to make a mean bruschetta."

"That will make your man very happy."

"I didn't do it for a man, I did it for myself."

He noted the defensive edge to her voice. "No man in your life, then?"

She set her jaw. "No."

He wondered why he liked that idea. "How many of you were in Italy?"

"Eight of us, including me."

He smiled. "The Italian men must not have known what hit them."

She shot him a sideways look. "Meaning?"

"Meaning I can only imagine the impression eight of you made on the locals…Tuscany will never be the same, I'm sure."

Her mouth curved. "My friend Jo was a big hit with the Italian men. She's a bit of a one-woman wrecking crew."

He gave her a considering look. "I'm sure she wasn't the only one."

She blinked. Looked away. *Shy,* he registered in astonishment. Were there actually any of those women left in Manhattan? It had been so long since he'd met one he'd thought they were extinct.

A loud creak split the air. He dropped the water, his heart slamming into his chest as he braced his hands on the floor. Isabel launched herself at him, wrapping her limbs around him. He held her close as the elevator swayed and groaned beneath them, his breath coming hard and fast.

What the hell?

CHAPTER TWO

"WHAT WAS THAT?"

Isabel screeched the words in his ear, wrapping her arms around his neck in a chokehold. The car rocked beneath them, but this time more gently, without the blood-curdling creak. He sucked in a breath. "It's just shifting," he told her, hoping that's all it was. "You're okay."

Her chest rose and fell rapidly against him. Seconds ticked by. The swaying slowed and then stopped. "Isabel, we're fine," he murmured, his heartbeat regulating as he brought his head down to hers. "I promise you, those cables don't break."

She drew in a deep breath, then another, stayed pressed against him. As his cortisol levels came down, his awareness of her skyrocketed. Her fingers were dug into his thigh, her light floral scent filling his nostrils. Her thoroughly touchable curves were plastered against him. And God help him, it was making him think improper thoughts. Like how much he'd appreciate those slender fingers wrapped around another part of his anatomy...

She drew back, her face chalk-white. Exhaled a long, agitated breath. Realized where her hand was. He struggled to wipe his expression clean as she lifted her horrified gaze to his, but he was pretty sure from the way her eyes widened and the speed with which she snatched her hand away, she'd known exactly where his head was at.

"I am so sorry," she murmured. But she was still in his lap, clutching his shoulder for dear life, and he was in severe danger of getting extremely turned on. Worse when she caught her plump bottom lip in her teeth and hell, he wished she wouldn't do that. He wanted to kiss her, and not the "Sunday walk in the park" variety.

Her pupils dilated, but she didn't go anywhere. He cleared his throat. "If this was your book," he drawled mockingly, "this'd be the part where I ravish you in the elevator, no?"

She was off his lap in a flash. She sat back against the wall, her shoulders pressed against the paneling. "Yes, well, that's why they have security cameras in elevators, don't they?" she pronounced stiffly. "To prevent that sort of behavior."

He had to stop himself from laughing out loud. "That sort of behavior? How very Victorian of you."

She fixed her eyes on the wall opposite her. "I think this elevator's getting to me."

She wasn't the only one. He waved a hand at her. "Think of it as extreme exposure therapy. After this you'll definitely be cured."

"Or I'll never set foot in an elevator again."

"Let's work toward the former." He gestured toward the can that had rolled to the corner of the elevator. "Put that on again."

She lifted it to her forehead. Stayed plastered against the wall like a modern painting, her white, pinched face a halo against the dark paneling. He cursed inwardly. He needed a distraction or this wasn't going to be pretty. *What in the world would he say to his sister Gabby, who was severely claustrophobic?*

"I have an idea," he suggested. "Let's play a game."

"A *game?*"

"You tell me something no one knows about you and I'll do the same."

She lifted a brow. "I'm channeling my sisters here," he offered grimly. "Humor me. If you go all panicky, it's not a good thing."

"Okay." She closed her eyes and leaned her head back against the wall. "In seventh grade, when Steven Thompson asked me to dance at the school mixer, I told him I'd sprained my ankle."

"You didn't like him?"

"I *adored* him." She opened her eyes. "I'd idolized him for years. But I thought my sister had put him up to it, like I was some kind of charity case, so I turned him down." She grimaced. "Turns out she hadn't."

"Ouch. So the poor guy got rejected for no good reason?"

She nodded. "I was persona non grata after that."

"And you females wonder why men aren't gallant anymore. We stick our necks out for *that*."

She gave him a wry look. "I hope you're using the royal 'we,' because I can't imagine you have ever been rejected in your entire life."

And that's where she was wrong. The one time he had been, the only time it had *mattered,* he'd been left for dead by the woman who'd meant everything to him.

"Nobody goes through life unscathed," he said roughly. "You should have given the guy a chance. Maybe you scarred him for life."

"Since he was dating Katy Fielding by the next Monday, I highly doubt it." Cynicism tainted her voice. "Okay, your turn."

He thought about it. And for some strange reason, he was dead honest. "I wish I'd made different decisions at times."

Her gaze sharpened on him. "Is that a general observation or something you'd care to elaborate on?"

Most definitely not. He'd shut the door on that part of his life a long time ago. Never to be opened again. "A general observation." He rested his gaze on her face. "Sometimes in life you're only given one shot. Use it wisely."

Her eyes stayed on his, assessing, inquisitive. Then she let it go with a sigh. "This interview I have tomorrow? I don't even know if I want the job. But it's a once-in-a-life-time kind of thing."

He frowned. "Why don't you want it? I assume it's a step up?"

"Fear," she said simply. "I'm afraid of what happens *if* I get it."

"Take it from me," he counseled, "fearing the unknown is far worse than facing it. I have no doubt you'll knock them dead, Isabel. Just be your quirky self."

She looked insulted. "Quirky?"

"Tell me it doesn't fit."

"Well…maybe just a bit."

She jumped as the phone rang. He pushed to his feet, walked over and picked up the receiver. But the news wasn't what he wanted to hear. *Two and a half hours.*

He hung up. "We have to sit tight for another couple of hours."

Isabel's face fell.

"Think on the bright side," he said, sliding down beside her and giving her a wicked look. "You can read me excerpts from your book. It was just getting good."

Exactly two and a quarter hours later, at about the time Izzie's flight was scheduled to take off from Heathrow, a rescue team arrived.

She and Alex stood to one side as the crew unscrewed a panel from the top of the car and dropped a ladder down, a burly, safety-cable laden rescuer climbing in moments later with two harnesses slung over his shoulder.

"Ready to get out of here?" he asked them, a wide grin splitting his face.

"You've no idea," Izzie murmured, flashing a sideways look at Alex. She really wasn't sure what she would have done without him. She had a sneaking suspicion she would have lost it completely.

"All right then," the technician said, strapping one of the harnesses around Izzie. "The next floor is about eight feet above us. We're going to climb up the ladder, out the top of the elevator and up onto the lobby floor." He snapped the harness into place and stepped back. "Keep moving, don't look down and you'll be fine."

Every limb in her body went ice cold. *They wanted her to climb through an elevator shaft?*

"I'll be right behind you," Alex said quietly. "It's mind over matter, Isabel."

Yes, but she didn't have a mind left! Her legs started to shake; her breath came in short, frantic bursts. "But what if—"

Alex took her hands in his, wrapping his fingers around hers. "There *is* no 'what if.' We're going to climb out of here and it's all going to be over, okay?"

She took a deep breath and let it out slowly, absorbing the quiet confidence in his voice, the warmth of his hands around hers. "You'll stay right behind me?"

He nodded.

"Okay." She pulled in another big breath and let go of his hands with a decisive movement. "Let's do it."

The technician strapped the other harness around Alex. Then they started up the ladder, Alex following Izzie. Her legs were shaking so hard she had to inject every bit of concentration she possessed into each step, her hands clutching the side of the ladder for balance.

"One step at a time," Alex murmured, anchoring his

hands firmly around her hips to steady her. "You're doing great."

She didn't *feel* great. Her heart was in her mouth, acid stung the back of her throat in the very real threat she might throw up, and she felt as if she was going to collapse in a puddle.

She forced herself to keep moving, her slow climb taking her up to where the ladder emerged from the car. She looked down. Gasped at the endless plunge into darkness.

"Don't look down," the technician said, turning around. "Keep going."

But her legs wouldn't move. "I can't," she whispered. "My legs, they—they're shaking so much I'm afraid I'll—"

Alex stepped up on the ladder behind her, his hands digging into her waist. "You can do this," he insisted firmly. "I'm right here and I'm not letting go. Just put one foot in front of the other and we'll be out of here in a minute."

The heat of his hands penetrated the thin cotton of her dress. Sank into her skin, warming her. Grounding her. "Mind over matter, Isabel," he whispered, his hands tightening. "Move with me."

She gritted her teeth and forced herself to focus on the strength of his hands around her waist. *He would not let her fall. He would keep her safe...*

She started climbing again, focusing only on putting one foot in front of the other as they emerged from the elevator, walked across the top of it and climbed the ladder toward the floor above. Step up, make sure her foot was securely on the rung, bring the other foot up. Repeat. She said it over and over again in her head as she did it, Alex's hands never leaving her waist. And then, someone was reaching down and grasping her by the arms and lifting her to solid ground.

Alex stepped up behind her, the look of grim relief on his face making her knees go weak. "You okay?"

She nodded. Swayed as her shaking knees turned to mush. He closed his arms around her and pulled her close, his chin coming down on top of her head. "It's okay," he murmured into her hair. "It's over."

Izzie had the strange feeling that once here, she might never want to leave. She buried her face in the rock-solid wall of his chest, her limbs shaking so hard she wondered if they'd ever stop.

"The paramedics are downstairs in the lobby, waiting to check you out," the burly rescuer said. "Sorry to say, the generator's still out, so you'll have to take the stairs."

Since Izzie never intended to get on another elevator in her life, that was just fine with her. But by the time they'd descended twenty-three flights of stairs and she'd gotten thoroughly poked and prodded by a young medic she was done.

"How many fingers am I holding up?" the medic asked, sticking up four.

She waved her hand at him. "I'm good, really. I hardly bumped it at all."

"It was a hard knock," Alex interjected, holding his cell phone away from his ear. "Let him do his job."

Izzie made a face. "Four," she sighed. "And I'm not seeing double...no halos, nothing..."

"Any dizziness?" he asked patiently.

"No."

"Okay, I think you're fine." He started packing up his kit. "But you should be watched for the next twenty-four hours to make sure you haven't suffered any kind of internal issues."

Izzie nodded. "No problem. I'm going to rebook myself on another flight to the States tonight so there'll be a whole planeload full of people ready to catch me if I keel over."

The medic frowned. "Flying isn't the best idea after an injury like that."

She shrugged. "I have no choice."

He gave her a long look. "Do you have someone in London you can stay with if that flight doesn't happen? Otherwise we can admit you to the hospital overnight for observation."

She blanched. Spending the night in the hospital wasn't an option. She *had* to get a flight. "I do," she lied. "Thanks so much for your help."

Alex was still on the phone when she picked up her bag and walked over to him. He held the phone to one side. "We can't get a flight to the States tonight. Give me your ticket and I'll have my assistant rebook you on something tomorrow morning."

Tomorrow? "There must be a flight tonight…a red-eye? I'll take a red-eye…"

He scowled. "By no flights, I mean no flights, Isabel."

Oh. She bit her lip, frantically sifting through the alternatives, but coming up with none. "Can you see if she can make it as early as possible tomorrow?" she asked, dragging her ticket out of her purse and handing it to him. "I have that interview in the morning."

He nodded, took the ticket and started rattling off the information into the phone. She left him to it, collapsing into one of the sterile-looking leather lobby chairs. If she caught a super early flight tomorrow she had a shot at making the interview, given the time difference. But she wasn't even sure overseas flights left that early in the morning. In fact she was pretty sure they didn't.

She swallowed hard and removed her fingernail from her mouth before she mangled it. This was a once-in-a-lifetime opportunity. What she'd been obsessively working toward for the past four years, coming into the studio at eight when most reporters didn't amble in until their 10:00 a.m. editorial meeting and working well past when most had left. She, a single girl in New York, had no per-

sonal life. Her job *was* her life. Which was fine, because
dating was like some type of ancient torture for her, and in
ten years she'd have a flourishing career to point to rather
than a series of America's worst matchmaking stories.

Her stomach dropped. She just hadn't expected to be
taking her big leap *now.*

An audition for an anchor job in the most high-pressure
media market in the country was a daunting task for even
the most experienced reporter. Ten times so for someone
like Izzie, who tended to burn out like the brightest star
when the stakes were the highest.

Been there, done that. She squeezed her eyes shut.
She was not that Izzie anymore—the terrified, unsure
eighteen-year-old who'd walked into that audition and
blown the biggest opportunity of her life. She would not
go back there. *Ever.* Particularly not when today, facing
her mortality, she'd suddenly had a crystal-clear vision
of how short life could be.

A shaky sigh escaped her as she leaned back into the
smooth leather. What was she doing, anyway? If those
emergency brakes hadn't deployed, she and Alex would
have been smashed to smithereens. Worrying about a job
was just nuts! But to be fair, she'd spent her whole life worrying. On a low, chronic level that couldn't be good for
a person. About keeping her job. About how she looked.
About what the future held. And right now, that seemed
like a very, very stupid way to live.

Alex dropped down in the chair beside her. "You okay?"

She nodded, her brain settling into an oddly lucid state.
"Actually," she said slowly, "I am."

He gave her a long look as if he was trying to decide if
she'd lost it. Then handed her ticket back with some scrib-
bles on it. "The best Grace could do was an eleven-thirty
tomorrow morning."

She did the calculation in her head. If she left here at

eleven-thirty, she'd land in New York around one-thirty. Maybe, just maybe, James could get the execs to stay later.

"Thank you," she murmured, sliding the ticket into her purse.

"No problem." His gaze sharpened on her face. "What did the paramedic say?"

"He says I'm fine…just to keep an eye on my head."

"You mean have someone keep an eye *on you*," he corrected. "For at least twenty-four hours probably. Any of those girlfriends of yours live in London?"

She shook her head. "I'm sure I'm fine. I'll just book a hotel, get a good night's sleep and it'll all be good."

His dark brows slanted together. "You don't fool around with a head injury, Isabel. It's serious stuff."

"I don't *have* a head injury. I have a bump on my head."

He gave her a dark look and raked his hand through his hair. "Give me a second. I'm going to see if I can find a nurse or someone who can keep an eye on you."

"*No* way I—*dammit*—" she cursed as he turned on his heel and strode off, already talking into his phone. She didn't need a nurse. She needed to get back to New York.

He came back five minutes later, his frown deeper. "My assistant couldn't find someone on such short notice."

"Well, that's it, then," she said, trying not to look relieved. "I'll make sure I keep an eye on myself and if I feel the slightest bit strange, I'll go to the hospital."

"No, you won't." His eyes darkened to a forbidding cobalt-blue. "I have plenty of space at my place in Canary Wharf. You can stay with me."

Her jaw dropped open. *Her stay with him at his place? Umm…no.* "That's very nice of you," she said, "but I can't impose like that."

"You need to be watched." He reached down and picked up her bag. "I don't know about you but I need a hot shower and something to eat. Let's go."

She shook her head. "Alex, I—"

"*Isabel.* I had a friend suffer a massive hemorrhage after he hit his head. We all thought he was fine. He died that night, at home *alone*."

"Oh." She stared at him, scared silly.

"*Exactly.* You've had a brutally traumatic day, you look like you're going to pass out, and I'm the one responsible for you whacking your head. So do me a favor and stay at my place so I don't have to spend the night worrying about you expiring in a hotel room."

And what was she supposed to say to that? Suddenly, staying alone in a hotel room seemed the height of stupidity. The thing was...despite how she knew instinctively she could trust him, despite how he'd taken care of her in that elevator, she didn't *know* him. He could be an ax murderer for all she knew. On the other hand, she knew *that* was ridiculous. As a reporter she lived by her instincts, and her instincts told her she could trust Alex.

"Just say yes," he muttered. "I'm out of patience."

She chewed on her lip. "All right. If you're sure it's not too much trouble..."

A rueful smile curved his mouth. "I have a feeling *you* are trouble, Isabel Peters. Having you stay with me is not."

But Izzie wasn't at all sure that was the truth. Seated in the low, sleek sports car Alex had parked in the underground lot, her pulse raced as fast as the high-performance engine rippling beneath her. It might have been the way she couldn't look at his muscular thighs on the low bucket seat beside her without remembering how that hard, male muscle had felt under her hands. Or the fact that despite his abrupt dismissal in the lobby earlier, there *had* been a spark between them in that elevator. Unless she was totally deluded...which had been known to happen when it came to her and men.

Tired of watching Izzie sit on the sidelines in Italy,

her girlfriend Jo had finally staged an intervention. "You have to engage with men to catch them," she'd advised caustically. "We aren't participating in immaculate conception here."

Izzie was clear on *that*. She just happened to be very, very bad at engaging.

She darted a sideways glance at the hard profile of the drop-dead-gorgeous man beside her. Could he actually be attracted to her? Or was she just kidding herself about that chemistry in the elevator? A man like that could have any woman he wanted. Why would he want vanilla when he could undoubtedly savor crème brûlée any day of the week?

The left and right sides of her brain warred with each other. Suddenly she was very, very tired of being Izzie the responsible. The girl who never took a risk. And it occurred to her that until she did, she might never know who she really was.

A flock of butterflies swooped through her stomach on a wild roller-coaster ride. Did she have the courage to find out tonight whether vanilla cut it? And if so, would it go down as the single most stupid thing she'd ever done? Or the best?

CHAPTER THREE

LEANDROS ALEXIOS CONSTANTINOU, Alex to all who knew him, stood on the terrace of his Canary Wharf penthouse at sunset, drinking in the spectacular light that blazed a golden path across the Thames. It never failed to take his breath away, this 270-degree panoramic vista of the city skyline and the river. Especially on a night like this, one of those warm, sultry summer evenings in London that made you think you'd be nuts to live anywhere else.

Worth every penny of the £2.5 million he'd paid for it, the peace and relaxation it brought him at the end of a fourteen-hour workday was usually foolproof. But not tonight. Not when all hell was breaking loose with his company back in New York, he was 3,500 miles away and his partner was an engineering genius, not a business brain. Not when a woman he was undoubtedly attracted to was showering in his guest room. The type of woman he'd vowed he wouldn't touch with a ten-foot pole after Jess had walked out on him.

He stared at the sky as its deep burnt-gold hue darkened into an exotic orange, then pink, streaks of color floating across the darkening horizon. He was more thrown by that free fall that could have plunged him and Izzie into oblivion than he'd care to admit. He supposed he wouldn't be human if he wasn't. But he didn't like where it was sending his mind. The uncharacteristic, impulsive things it was making him do. Like bringing a chaotic bundle of nerves named Isabel Peters home with him.

Truthfully, though, he hadn't had much choice. It was his fault she'd hit her head. He couldn't let her stay alone in a hotel room—not after losing his former teammate Cash as he had. And without a nurse to look after her, responsibility fell squarely in his lap.

Speaking of which… He turned and cocked his head toward the open windows. Izzie had been in that shower forever. All he needed was for her to collapse and drown. She'd certainly been pale enough.

Hell. He strode inside, stopped outside the bedroom he'd put her in and opened the door. "Are you okay in there?" he yelled.

"I'm good," she called back over the sound of running water. "Getting out now."

He shut the door, *firmly,* as his head went directly to an image of her naked and slippery under his hands, foam highlighting those curves.

He went back outside and switched on the lights. A whisper-soft breeze picked up as he walked to the edge of the terrace and rested his forearms on the top of the concrete wall. At least she was keeping his mind off Taylor Bayne, who'd taken his European expansion plans and dismantled them with a flick of his Rolex-clad wrist this morning.

Christós. His gut twisted in a discomforting reminder of that disaster of a boardroom this morning at Blue Light Interactive. He'd known something was up the minute he'd shaken the normally gregarious CEO's hand and the other man had studiously avoided his gaze. Waved him to the massive dark-stained table, where the fractures in the deal had started to appear, one by one. All of a sudden things that hadn't been issues before became major sticking points and Bayne was backpedaling faster than a quarterback who'd run out of room.

He let out a string of curses. What had made Bayne do a complete 180 like that? And how had he misread him so badly? For a man whose life had been a series of carefully orchestrated steps to take him where he was going, it was disconcerting to say the least. For Alex, there were no missteps. No deviations. No distractions. Only the master plan.

When he was six, growing up in sports-obsessed New York City, he'd decided he was going to be a famous football player. Never mind his father's plans for him to take over C-Star Shipping as the family's only male heir. For Alex it had only ever been about football. From the first time he'd held that piece of rawhide in his hands playing in the backyard with the neighborhood boys, he'd known it was the only thing he ever wanted to do.

A successful high school career and a brilliant Hail Mary pass to win his college team a national championship made his dream of playing professional football a reality. He got an offer from a New York team. Had been touted as the next big thing. That was when his father had hit the roof…this "hobby" of Alex's had to stop. It was time for him to be a man and join the ranks of tough, brilliant Constantinou businessmen.

His hands tightened around the railing, the dusky, early-evening sky transforming into the dark Boston bar where his father had sat him down with a bottle of whiskey and hell in his eyes. Tonight they were going to hash this out, he'd told Alex. Didn't he realize the shame he was bringing on the Constantinou name by abandoning his birthright for a frivolous career like American football?

Thud. Thud. Thud. The sound of the bottle hitting the worn wooden table was indelibly imprinted in his head. The bitter taste of the whiskey he'd never liked lingered in his mouth even now. His father's harsh, nicotine-stained voice as he brushed aside Alex's quietly issued plea. *You've achieved your dream. Let me go after mine.* Hristo's reply, sharp as a knife. *Sign that contract, Alexios, and you are no longer a part of this family.*

His heart contracted, his knuckles shining white against the concrete barrier. He'd been so hurt, so angry, he'd signed the three-year contract the next day. And true to his word, his father had disowned him—had never come to another game.

He'd played incredibly well—become a superstar. He'd made an insane amount of money. But he'd never earned his father's respect. And then, on one fateful evening, in the third year of his career, it had all been taken away from him. He'd had to learn what it was like to be a survivor. To hit rock bottom, claw his way out and start all over again.

Sophoros had been the result of that single-minded determination. Alongside his best buddy from college, brilliant software programmer Mark Isaacs, he'd built America's most successful computer gaming company.

His mouth tightened, his fingers flexing around the concrete. It would be over his dead body that he'd watch Sophoros fail because of a greedy, lazy, half-talented former employee out for a free ride.

He stared up at the night sky, Venus making her first sparkling appearance. Calling to him like a signpost. *No deviations. No distractions.* He should be thinking about the mess that was waiting for him back in New York. Figuring out his game plan. Not worrying about what the hell Isabel Peters was still doing in the shower when she'd said ten minutes ago she was getting out.

"Alex—this is unbelievable!"

He turned around to find Isabel standing barefoot behind him, wearing the dress of his sister's he'd found in the spare bedroom.

His first reaction was that his sister didn't look like that in that dress. His second was that he was a dead man.

Still far too pale, her dark hair and eyes shone in the

early evening light, set off by the cappuccino-colored dress. She'd put her hair up in a ponytail, her face bare of makeup except for a berry-colored gloss on her lips. Innocent. Harmless enough. The dress that hugged every inch of her curvy figure, emphasizing high breasts, a narrow waist and gently rounded hips, was not. She had the kind of body that made a man want to put his hands all over her, he thought distractedly. In no particular order.

Her blush as he raised his gaze to hers wasn't something he'd seen on a woman in a long time. "I think I might be a size bigger than your sister."

Deciding there was no appropriate response to that question he could verbalize, he cleared his throat and kept his eyes firmly focused on her face. "You're white as a ghost."

She pressed her hands to her cheeks. "I feel much better after the shower."

"You need a stiff drink." *Theos*, he needed a stiff drink.

She followed him inside, perching herself on a stool at the solid mahogany bar while he searched for and found a bottle of brandy.

"Wow. This place is fabulous."

He turned around and studied her. It was an observation. An appreciation of the luxury they were standing in rather than the typical "I want this place to be mine" expression he'd seen on the faces of the few women he'd brought up here.

"Thanks," he nodded, uncorking the bottle and pouring an inch in one glass and double in the other. He handed her the smaller one. "It was a good investment given the London real estate market."

She wrapped her fingers around the crystal tumbler, their slim grace and perfectly manicured nails drawing his eye. "Alex— I—" She stopped, looking hesitant. "I don't know how to say thank you for everything you've done for me today."

"Don't." He screwed the lid back on the bottle and returned it to the shelf. "It was nothing."

"It *was*," she insisted, those big brown eyes of hers sweeping hesitantly over him as he turned back to her. "I think I would have completely lost it if it wasn't for you."

He shrugged. "Phobias are powerful things."

"Still," she said, lifting her chin and holding his gaze. "Thank you."

"You're welcome." He nodded toward her glass. "Drink up. The brandy will help."

She took a sip. Made a face. "Must be an acquired taste."

He shot her an amused look. "Are you calling me old, Isabel?"

Twin dots of pink stained her cheeks. "Hardly. You're what…thirty?"

"Thirty-two. And you?"

"Twenty-five." She lifted her shoulders in an attempt at a sophisticated shrug. "Seven years…that's not so much of a difference."

"You'd be surprised what you can pack into those seven years," he said drily. He sat his drink on the bar and walked to the shelf of CDs in the living room. "I've ordered some dinner from the restaurant downstairs. I thought we could have it on the terrace."

"I'd love that. The view's amazing."

"Then I'm putting you to bed." *Unfortunately not his.*

"I'm so wired I'm not sure I can sleep."

He turned to face her. She seemed incredibly vulnerable sitting there, a restless energy emanating from her he found mirrored in himself. It had been one hell of a day. "The brandy and a good meal will solve that. You're probably running on adrenaline now."

"I think I am."

He turned back to the CDs and scanned the titles. "Any preference in music?"

"I listen to everything."

"Classical?"

"Yes." She smiled as he looked over at her. "My dad's a music professor at Stanford. I was brought up listening to that stuff."

"Did he make you play every instrument known to man?"

"Yes, until he discovered I had absolutely no artistic talent whatsoever."

His lips curved. "He must have been crushed."

"I hated it," she said, shaking her head. "I'm all thumbs when it comes to anything creative."

Did that include the bedroom? he wondered. He wasn't so caught up with creativity. But natural passion was a must.

Christós He forced his gaze back to the music in front of him. He really had to get his mind out of the gutter. Away from the fact that every time she swung those slim legs on that stool, he wondered what they would feel like wrapped around him. Whether she'd dig her heels into his back while he took her slow and deep and—

Whoa. He slapped the CD he was looking at back on the shelf and raked a hand through his hair. Had it been too long since he'd had a woman? Was that what this was all about? What had it been? Two, three months? He'd been so buried in the Blue Light Interactive deal he hadn't had two seconds to even think about a woman, let alone bed one.

Or maybe it had just been three hours stuck in an elevator fighting an attraction that seemed to be growing by the minute?

He stared at the CDs. Spanish...he was going with Spanish. He grabbed a compilation of adagios and slid it into the player. The haunting strains of a lone guitar filled the room.

"I wouldn't have pegged you as the classical guitar type," she said as he walked back over to join her at the bar.

He aimed a reproving glance at her. "Stereotyping me, Isabel? You were questioning my reading taste earlier..."

Her mouth twisted. "You're right. My mistake. You're just a bit of a closed book, unlike me and my big mouth."

He shrugged and picked up his drink. "You know the basics. I'm a native New Yorker, run my own company..."

"The details are overwhelming," she said drily. "The accent is Greek?"

He nodded. "I was born in the US to Greek parents. But I spent my summers in the islands."

"Where'd you go to school?"

"Boston College."

"Why Boston when you had all those schools in New York?"

"Sports and their business program." She didn't need to know he'd gone on full scholarship. That as far as the university brass had been concerned, he'd been the closest thing to a savior their football program had ever seen.

"Ah, a typical male," she teased. "The sports bug."

"The natural order of things," he agreed with a lazy smile, tilting his glass toward her. "Where did you go to school?"

"Columbia."

"But you aren't from New York." He lifted a brow. "I can hear the faint traces of a Southern drawl."

She shook her head. "California. Palo Alto. I moved to New York to go to school."

"Are your family still out West?"

"Just my dad. My parents are separated. My mom lives in New York and my sister—" her lips curved "—well, she's a nomad. She models all over the world. I never know what city I'm calling her in."

He took a sip of his drink, feeling the smooth brandy burn its way down his throat. "How old were you when your parents separated?"

A rueful glint lit her eyes. "It's kind of like the divorce that never happened."

Sounded like hell to him. At least his mother had made up her mind and gotten out. He folded his arms and tucked his drink against his chest, resting his gaze on her face. "How so?"

She shrugged. "My mother's an actress. Used to the bright lights and the big city. She was always leaving for shoots, for extended appearances in London in the theater...and eventually she just stopped coming home. I think she decided one day that we and Palo Alto just weren't exciting enough for her."

He frowned. "Would I know her?"

She hesitated, looked as if this was the last thing she wanted to talk about. "Her name is Dayla St. James."

A vague recollection of a dark-haired bombshell floated into his head. "Was she in a wartime movie? Played a woman whose husband never came back from the front?"

She nodded. "That's her. Kind of ironic, isn't it?"

"Kind of." He studied her face. "You don't look much like her."

"So she likes to tell me."

He drew his brows together. "I didn't mean you aren't beautiful, Isabel. Surely many men have told you that you are."

Her gaze dropped to her brandy. She swirled it around the glass. "You don't need to humor me. My mother is a gorgeous movie star...my sister is a glamorous international model. I get it. I've been living with it my whole life."

He held his tongue and counted to five. Anything he said here could and would be used against him. He had three sisters. He knew how their minds worked. "You should have more confidence in yourself," he said flatly. "You're a beautiful girl."

She pressed her lips shut. Stared at him.

His phone rang. *Thank the Lord for small favors.*

"Can you set the table while I take this?" He pulled his phone out of his pocket. "Plates are in the cupboard beside the sink."

His partner Mark's cheerful voice boomed over the line. "Grace told me what happened. You okay, man? That must have been one hell of a ride."

"This whole day's been one hell of a ride." Alex elbowed his way through the door to his study. "But yes, I'm fine."

"Blue Light wasn't good?"

He sank down on the corner of his desk. "Something happened between our last meeting and today. Bayne was backing off left, right and center."

"I think I have the explanation for you," Mark drawled. "And you aren't going to like it."

An uneasy feeling snaked its way up his spine. "What?"

"Taylor Bayne met with Frank Messer last week in London."

Alex uttered a low curse. "How do you know?"

"Do you really want me to answer that?"

He grimaced. "No." His partner, who had seen him through the darkest of times when his career ended and was still his only close confidant, was a programming genius. Which, translated, meant he was a hacker who could crack anything. "So what were they talking about?"

"Don't know." He heard his partner take a sip of something, which was undoubtedly coffee. He was addicted to it. "But you can be damn sure it had something to do with today."

"He's laying the groundwork for the court case." It was all starting to fall into place. Having watched Sophoros's stock value skyrocket, his ex-director of software, Frank Messer, was getting greedy, figuring he'd let them off far too lightly when they'd parted ways seven years ago. So now he was taking them to court claiming he should have been given a much bigger settlement the first time around. And apparently was trying to alienate the people Sophoros did business with.

He slammed his fist against the desk. "*Christós,* Mark, we should have buried him while we had the chance."

"Truer words have never been said. The lawyers think we have a hell of a fight on our hands."

Great. Just what he needed to hear after this fiasco of a day. "I need the jet, Mark. I've got to get out of here."

"Way ahead of you, buddy. Grace has them working on it tonight. She'll give you a call in the morning with an update."

"Good." His twenty-three-year-old PA was a formidable force way beyond her years. She'd have that jet in the air tomorrow morning if it was humanly possible.

"Alex…" Isabel's voice rang out, a panicked, shrill sound that made him stiffen.

"Is that a woman's voice?" His partner's tone deepened to one of incredulity. "Seriously, Alex, I don't know how you do it. You're grounded in London for a few hours and you have a woman there already?"

"It's a long story," Alex said shortly, the hairs on the back of his neck standing up as he beat it toward the kitchen. "I gotta go. I'll talk to you in the morning."

"I can't wait to hear it." His partner's voice dripped with amusement. "Enjoy yourself, buddy."

He disconnected the call, arriving in the kitchen just in time to see Isabel standing on top of the counter, her hands pressed against a row of wineglasses that had toppled over and threatened to crash to the floor.

"What *are* you doing?" He hoisted himself up beside her and grabbed a handful of the glasses.

She pushed the rest back onto the shelf. "I'm sorry. I—I just thought we'd want the wineglasses. You had that bottle of wine on the counter and then I got a little dizzy and knocked one over and there was this chain reaction and—"

Visions of an exhausted Isabel falling and cracking her head open on the hard tile let loose a string of curses from Alex. He jumped down to the floor, reached up, wrapped his hands around her waist and lifted her down, setting her bottom on the counter. "Did you really think this was a good idea?"

She pushed some stray curls out of her face, her cheeks turning a bright red. "I didn't feel dizzy before I went up there."

He shook his head. "You need to eat." And if he were a smart man he would back away right now. Back away from the eye-level temptation staring back at him.

"Alex...?" She sank her teeth into her lower lip and gave him one of those wide-eyed looks.

"What?" he asked roughly.

"Am I a total idiot or do you want to kiss me?"

He blinked. Closed his eyes. He never lied. *Ever.* But right about now it seemed like a good idea. "Can I pass on that one?"

"Alex."

He opened his eyes.

"My friend Jo told me I never engage." She bit down harder into her lip. "With men, I mean. Which is why I'm asking the question. To see if I'm seriously deluded or not."

He bit out a curse he hadn't uttered since his college days. "I'm not the right guy for you, Isabel."

She gave him a determined look. "I'm talking about a kiss. Not the rest of our lives."

He shook his head. "Same answer."

She hesitated, swallowed hard. "You said in the elevator that it's better to face the unknown than fear it. What if you're my modern-day Steven Thompson?"

"This time you *should* walk away," he muttered.

"Please answer the question," she pleaded. "Otherwise I'm going to feel like a total idiot. Good or bad, I can take it."

He pressed his hands to his temples. It'd taken a lot of nerve to ask that question. And it had been *his* mistake in ever admitting he found her attractive. "Yes," he conceded finally, "I want to kiss you but—"

"Alex." The tension in her face slid away. "Get on with it, will you?"

"This is an insanely bad idea," he groaned. But he was already stepping into her and lowering his mouth to the lush temptation in front of him. Because really, how much would one kiss hurt? "You just about passed out up there," he murmured against her lips.

"I'm fine," she said, tilting her chin up so their lips touched more firmly. Then the insanity of the day took over and he brought his mouth down on hers in a sensual tasting that explored every centimeter of her undeniably sweet lips.

His brain told him this was a bad idea even as he reached up and cupped the back of her head to change the angle of the kiss. Deeper, harder it went until she sighed and melted into him, curling her hands into his shirt. He was not unaware of how easy it would be to slip her panties off, wrap her legs around his waist, release himself and take her right there, right now. Exactly as he'd imagined it a few minutes ago...

Except he was a sane man. She hadn't eaten. She was dizzy. And she most definitely did not know the score.

He lifted his mouth from hers and gently pushed her away from him. "You need to eat," he said roughly. "This has been quite a day."

Myriad emotions flickered through those dark eyes of hers. "Alex, I—"

He put a finger to her mouth. "No more talking. Not one word until we eat."

"But—" The doorbell interrupted her.

"That's dinner." He ran his hands through his hair and straightened his clothing. "Go outside and sit down. I'll bring everything out."

She gave him one last, long look, then pressed her lips together and slid off the counter. He cursed under his breath as he watched her walk out of the room. He'd been right. He was a dead man.

Izzie focused on forking the small amount of food she thought she could consume into her mouth at the small candlelit table Alex had set on the terrace. The herbed pasta was delicious, but it was hard to eat when her heart was still pounding and her hands trembling so much negotiating a fork seemed like a new and highly complex activity. And why wouldn't it when she had literally jumped into the deep end and invited the most spectacularly good-looking man she'd ever met to kiss her—and he had! Not to mention the fact that the kiss had been the most incredible of her life and all she could think about was experiencing more of the bone-meltingly delicious heat that had coursed through her veins. It was as if every nerve ending in her body had been switched on for the first time and she wasn't sure whether to revel in it or be completely terrified of what she was feeling.

She swallowed hard, forced down the food. The fact that

she'd been right—that Alex was attracted to her—made her head feel as though it was going to explode. Maybe Jo was right. Maybe it had been her defensive attitude that had turned men off in the past and not the few extra pounds she'd been carrying. Which had always been her excuse.

She took another sip of the rich, full cabernet that was going a long way to mellowing her out. But the wine didn't seem to be having the same effect on Alex, who'd glowered at her throughout the entire meal—as if she'd committed a crime rather than simply kissed him.

She risked a quick glance at him. He was still watching her with that same implacable frown on his face, that penetrating blue gaze of his impossible to read. And it occurred to her she hadn't fully thought through her plan. She had the mind-numbing confirmation that he was attracted to her. The question now was what was she going to do about it?

Her heart pounding in her chest, she set her fork down with an abrupt movement, and the sound of metal clattering against fine china echoed in the still night air.

He gave her half-empty plate a narrowed glance. "That's all you're going to eat?"

"It was delicious, thank you. I think that's about all I can handle."

"All right." He laid his fork down with a deliberate movement and pushed his plate away. "Let's talk about what happened."

Gladly. She took another sip of her wine to fortify herself and set the glass down.

"That kiss shouldn't have happened."

She was ready for that one. "Why not?"

"I'm much more experienced than you, Isabel. I'm not interested in relationships—in fact, mine never last longer than a few months, and the women I date are well aware of that."

"So?"

He did a double take at the belligerent note in her voice. "You're also probably still in shock from what happened today."

"I'm absolutely fine," she countered. "In fact, I feel like I have more clarity right now than I've ever had in my life."

He sat back in his chair, his gaze on her face. "What kind of clarity?"

She twisted the stem of her wineglass on the table, watching the bloodred liquid shimmer in the candlelight. "That was my worst fear today. Facing it—getting through it—" she paused, looking up at him "—it's made me realize how much of my life I've lived in fear...how many times I've not gone after what I wanted because I was afraid I wouldn't get it or it would explode in my face."

He gave a wary nod. "That's a good realization."

She shook her head. "I'm not looking for a relationship, Alex." A husky laugh escaped her. "In fact, that's the last thing I need right now."

His eyes narrowed. "Then what *are* you looking for?"

"I don't want to live with any more regrets."

He shook his head, a wry smile curving his lips. "You're twenty-five, Isabel. How many regrets can you have?"

She took a deep breath, meeting his gaze head-on. "I will regret it if I walk away from tonight without exploring the attraction that's between us."

A muscle jumped in his jaw. He sat there completely silent, staring at her. "I'm not sure you know what you're doing."

She shook her head. "I know exactly what I'm doing."

A long moment passed; it might have been four, five seconds, she wasn't sure. All she knew was that she was holding her breath, sure at one point he was going to reject her. The warm night air pressed so heavily against her lungs she thought they would burst. And then something shifted, morphed on the air between them. And she got her answer in the darkening of his eyes.

He stood up and held out a hand. "Let's go enjoy the view, then."

CHAPTER FOUR

THE SULTRY NIGHT AIR, so quiet and still as they stood at the railing and took in the cityscape, seemed to envelop Izzie in a world so far removed from her normal life that she could almost believe that it was. That it was just the two of them who existed and this incredible panoramic view of London with its lights twinkling across the water had been created for them and them alone.

That what felt like a defining moment in her life was utterly, absolutely the right thing to do.

"You must spend so much time out here," she said to Alex, shaking her head. "It's breathtaking."

A wry smile curved his mouth. "It's my second office when I'm in London. When the weather is good…"

Izzie tried to focus as he pointed out the London landmarks to her, stopping to give her a bit of history on each, but the anticipation coursing through her veins made her feel weak-kneed. Light-headed.

"What's that?" She pointed at a series of small structures stretching across the water on either side of a bridge.

"That's the Thames barrier."

"Those white things that look like little Sydney Opera Houses?"

He moved behind her and directed her fingers toward the circular structures she'd been looking at. "Those."

Her temperature spiked dramatically as the hard, warm length of him brushed against her back. "Right," she murmured. "That's what I thought."

He didn't move away, but dropped his hands to the railing instead, resting them on either side of her. Her heartbeat sped up.

"Flooding has become an issue for London over the years. Water levels have been continuously rising and threatening the city. In one of the big floods, many years back, hundreds of people died."

"Really?" She could barely breathe, so distracted was she by the pulses of electricity his big, warm body was sending through hers.

"Are you listening?" He moved his lips closer to her ear. "There's going to be a quiz later, you know."

"Later?" She gave up all pretext of paying attention when his hand brushed the weight of her hair aside and he set his lips to the sensitive skin at the nape of her neck.

"Mmm…one kiss was not nearly enough, Isabel."

Her legs felt as though she'd been through one too many Spin classes. Weaker still when he pressed his mouth to the sensitive junction between her neck and shoulder. The question was, did she have the guts to go through with this? For all her bravado, she'd only ever had one lover—and not a good one at that—in her college boyfriend. What if she disappointed Alex with her lack of experience?

"I can see the smoke coming out of your ears," he murmured against her skin. "Stop thinking so much."

Which was exactly what she needed to do. She'd been thinking so much her entire life she felt as though she'd been watching it from the sidelines. And if there was anything this crazy day had taught her, it was that life was tenuous. Fragile. And it could be taken from you at any moment. So best to jump in and take your chances.

Taking a deep breath, she turned around and met the

questioning intensity of his deep blue gaze. Felt the heat—
oh dear Lord—the heat of those sizzling good looks up
close. The hard planes of his face that made him look formidable...until he smiled. That square jaw with its delicious indentation that made a woman want to put her lips
to it. The sensuous, full mouth... It was all a bit heart-
stopping.

And incredibly difficult to find her voice. In the end,
she didn't try. Just went up on tiptoes, lifted her chin, and
brought her lips a hairbreadth away from his in silent invitation.

Something flickered in his eyes. "Can I ask you a question?"

She nodded.

"Are those glasses for distance?"

She blinked. "Yes."

He reached up and plucked them from her face. "Then
I guess you won't be needing them." Her breath caught,
strangled in her throat as he set the glasses down on the
railing beside them. "This is about to get up close and
very personal."

Oh God. Her heart raced in her chest as he reached up
and captured her jaw in his palm, his gaze following his
thumb as it swept across her cheek and over the surface
of her bottom lip. "You have the most amazing mouth,"
he murmured, exerting a slight downward pressure so she
opened for him. "It's the kind of mouth a man couldn't re-
sist even if he wanted to."

Which was good because if he didn't kiss her right now,
she was going to die. Transfixed, she watched as he lowered his head, her lashes fluttering down as he angled his
mouth over hers in a caress so light, so sensuous, it made
her whole body go weak. Her hands came up to balance her
against the hard wall of his chest, a sigh escaping her throat

as he explored, tasted every centimeter of her lips, getting intimately acquainted in a way that made her toes curl.

The kiss seemed to go on forever and ever, a leisurely tasting that neither of them seemed inclined to end. "This needs to go," he muttered, reaching up to unclasp her hair so it fell in a heavy swath down her back.

He drew back and raked his gaze over her. "You also have the most sensational hair."

"I almost cut it all off recently." She'd thought it might look more professional on-camera.

He reached out to twist one of her curls around his finger. "Don't ever, *ever* do that."

She smiled. "What is it about men and hair?"

He wound the curl tight, then let it go. "It's great fodder for fantasies...I've been imagining what it would look like spread across the white satin sheets of that big lonely bed of mine in there."

Words. She knew there were words in the English language. But the thought of him fantasizing about them in bed together wiped them clean from her head.

It didn't matter, though, because he was lifting her up on her tiptoes again, tunneling his hands in her hair to cup the back of her head, his sinful expression as his mouth came down on hers telling her he intended to indulge every minute of that fantasy in short order.

This time his kisses were of the hot, openmouthed variety that left her gasping. He made her give back everything he was offering her, hotter and hotter until she felt as though she were going to combust.

By the time his tongue traced the trembling fullness of her bottom lip, dipping inside and tangling erotically with hers, she wanted all he had to offer and more. She tipped her head back and took him in, giving him full access to her mouth. The intimacy of the kiss set her blood on fire.

He nudged her backward against the cool, hard concrete of the wall, his muscular thigh sliding between hers at the same time he dragged his lips down to explore the sensitive skin at the base of her throat. "Your pulse is racing..." he murmured against her skin.

She fought to control a shiver than ran through her as he trailed his lips across her collarbone to the soft skin of her shoulder. "I'm a little—"

"Excited?" he finished, a wicked smile curving his lips as he raised his blue gaze to hers. "But we're only just getting started, sweetheart."

Izzie squeezed her eyes shut, heat flooding her cheeks. Alex's low laughter danced across the night air as he bent to press his lips to her shoulder, his teeth nipping lightly at the tender skin as he slid his fingers under the strap of her dress and eased it off her shoulder. Izzie grabbed hold of the wall on either side of her as his lips worked their way over to her other shoulder and dispensed with the other strap.

Her eyes flew open as he eased the material of her dress away from her skin, pushing it down over the swell of her breasts to reveal the lacy bra she wore underneath. His soft curse made her cheeks burn anew. She lifted her hands to cover herself, a bout of extreme self-consciousness overwhelming her.

"Isabel..." He slid his fingers under her chin and brought her gaze back up to meet his. "You are so gorgeous you blow my mind."

She let her hands fall away then, the heat in his gaze holding her, drawing her back in. He lowered his head until his mouth brushed against hers. Took her lips in a hard kiss that wiped every last insecurity from her head. Her bones went liquid as he demonstrated how much he wanted her, demanding her response as he took her deeper. And she gave herself up to the sensations he was creating, gasping as his big hands came up to cup the weight of her breasts.

"Beautiful," he murmured, skating his thumbs over her nipples and bringing them to instant, hard, aching erectness under the lace of her bra. She squeezed her eyes shut at the erotic image, digging her nails harder into the concrete. He bent to take a lace-covered peak in his mouth, while his fingers continued to tease the other. The liquid heat invading her body sped to her core. Melted her from the inside out. His tongue flicked and teased her nipple, the sensation so exquisitely good she forgot where she was, everything but how good what he was doing to her felt.

He stopped playing then, taking her lace-covered nipple deep inside his mouth, sucking and tugging on it with his teeth until a slow, dull ache started deep inside her. An ache she'd never felt before.

"Alex," she murmured helplessly, not knowing what was happening to her, unsure of what to do with this extreme pleasure he was giving her.

He shifted his attention to her other breast. "Good?" he murmured, taking the hard peak inside his mouth.

"Mmm…" Her case of no words was rapidly getting worse. She shifted restlessly against his hard thigh, searching for some kind of relief. Sucking deeply on her nipple, he ran his hands down over her hips, found the hem of her dress and dragged it up, so he could settle his thigh between her bare legs. *Oh…* Izzie gasped at the sensation of his cloth-covered thigh rasping against her skin. It felt unbearably intimate and oh so good pressed against the damp heat of her. And she realized exactly what he'd given her. His hard muscles were the perfect antidote to the burning ache building inside of her. More so when she rocked against them and tiny sparks of electricity zigzagged through her.

"*Theos*, you're going to be the end of me," he muttered, lifting his head from her breast to stare at her, hot color staining his cheekbones.

The fact that he was as aroused as she was made every nerve ending quiver. Gave her a confidence she'd never known she had as she met his gaze, letting him see exactly how much she wanted him. He slid his thigh from between hers, pulled her against him, and bent slightly to run his hands up the back of her thighs. She drew in a breath as he cupped her bottom, arching her into him until she could feel his hard arousal. *Good Lord.* Her throat went dry. He felt big and hard and...intimidating. Very intimidating.

Biting down her apprehension, she held her breath as he traced the edge of her panties over the curve of her bottom. "A thong," he muttered huskily in her ear. "You really are trying to be the ultimate male fantasy, aren't you?"

Her cheeks burned as he brought his hands around to the front of her, pushing her back so he could trail his fingers teasingly along the front edge of her panties until he reached the damp warmth between her thighs.

His gaze speared hers. "Tell me what you want."

Her legendary ability to talk failed her. How was she supposed to tell him that when she didn't even *know* what she wanted? Her ex had never been into touching her *there*. Had never been interested in anything more than his own pleasure.

Alex saved her, his eyes darkening with amusement. "How about this?" he murmured, sliding his fingers against her through the thin material, pushing it into her so he could feel the damp evidence of her arousal.

Izzie closed her eyes.

He laughed softly, his thumb moving up to rotate against the hard nub at the center of her. "I love that I can turn you on like this."

The wicked things he was doing with his thumb wiped her embarrassment clean from her head. She gripped the concrete wall harder with her hands, head thrown back, eyes closed as she gave herself in to the sensations he was administering.

"Alex," she murmured, the need in her voice shocking her.

"Tell me what you want," he encouraged softly.

"Anyone could see us here…"

"They'd have to have a telescope."

What if they did? She stopped caring when he pressed his lips to her neck and increased the pressure of his thumb against her. "Touch me," she pleaded desperately, her hips rotating against his hand.

"But I am…"

"You know what I mean."

The first slide of his fingers against her hot, swollen flesh was the single most pleasurable thing she'd felt in her adult life. Her knees went weak and she leaned against the wall for support. "*Theos,* you are so turned on," he groaned, moving his thumb up to the hard button of her arousal, this time without any barrier. "This what you want, Iz?" he murmured, beginning that maddening set of circles against her that was building an unbearable tension in her body. Izzie bit back the moan that rose in her throat, convinced she wasn't going to make it through this. Every nerve in her body felt as if it was centered under his fingers, and it felt so good she was crazy with it.

"*Yes.*" Twisting restlessly against him, she begged him for more, faster, anything that would help her deal with the insane ache he was building in her.

"And this?" There was a raspy edge to his voice as he slid one of his long fingers inside her. Izzie sank her teeth into her lip, feeling her body accommodate the intrusion. Then the incredible feeling of him stroking her, stretching her, sent her to a whole other stratosphere.

"Alex," she heard herself say brokenly, no longer in control of anything she was doing or feeling.

"More?" he asked, sliding another of those pleasure-inducing fingers into her, waiting while she accepted him. This time her gasp rang out on the night air as he set a rhythm that was taking her somewhere she knew she wanted to go. *Now*. Before she shattered into a million little pieces.

"Please," she begged him, not knowing what to do, what to ask for to make it happen.

He bent his head to hers, dragging his mouth across her swollen lips. "Go with it, Iz," he urged in a soft, husky voice that inflamed her senses. "Let yourself go."

"I don't— *Oh,*" she breathed against his lips as he slid his thumb against the center of her while his fingers continued to slide in and out of her, increasing their rhythm now until there was such an unbearable tension focused between her legs she thought she would scream.

Then, with one last maddening press of his thumb against her, he took her over the edge, the most exquisite wave of pleasure washing over her, stiffening her limbs and focusing every nerve in her body on the white-hot pleasure radiating out from the center of her. She shoved a fist into her mouth, terrified she *would* scream out as he kept his fingers pressed to her to extract every last second of her orgasm.

Her first. The mind-shattering pleasure soaked her senses as she came slowly back to reality and found Alex watching her, the intent look on his face telling her he'd guessed it had been exactly that.

"That's never happened to you before."

"No."

"Are you a virgin?"

She shook her head.

The tension in the hard set of his jaw slackened.

"Would it have mattered?"

"Of course it would have. I told you I don't get complicated with women, Isabel."

"And a virgin is more complicated?" She didn't get it. She was one step removed from being one herself, and it didn't feel complicated.

He shrugged. "Of course they are. Women always want to romanticize their first sexual experience. Didn't you?"

She shook her head. "My ex-boyfriend was more interested in satisfying himself than me. Not that we want to dredge up stories of past lovers," she added lightly, desperately afraid he might ask her exactly how many men she'd slept with.

"No, we don't," he agreed, bending down to slide an arm under her knees so he could swing her up into his arms. "I can think of much better things to do with the time."

Izzie had never been carried by a man. Which was a shame, really, because she felt so delicate and feminine in Alex's arms as he carried her inside she decided it was an experience every woman should have at least once in her life.

He set her down on the cool hardwood floor of the utterly masculine master bedroom he'd shown her on the tour earlier. The bedroom featured the same floor-to-ceiling views the rest of the penthouse had, decorated in rich, muted tones that perfectly reflected the man himself.

She looked around as he flicked on some lamps. "No curtains."

He gave her an amused look. "You can't see in the glass, only out."

Which made it the perfect venue for an incredibly erotic sexual experience, she decided, trying not to jump out of her skin as he moved behind her and set his teeth to her shoulder. "Was that your idea or the builder's?"

He laughed softly. "The builder's. Were you imagining me creating some sort of seduction pad?"

She shrugged, jealousy flaring inside her despite the fact that she had absolutely no claim on him. "I'm sure you've brought more than a few women up here."

His fingers moved to the clasp of her bra. "Are you asking?"

She made herself shake her head. Except when he unhooked it with extreme ease and flipped it to the floor, she thought maybe she should.

He slid his arms around her and cupped her breasts. "I'm a pretty choosy guy when it comes to female companionship."

She gasped as his thumbs brought her nipples back to erectness. She was sure he could afford to be.

The soft rasp of her zipper came next. Cool air hit her skin as he pushed the dress over her hips and it fell to the floor, leaving her clad only in her thong. She swallowed hard as he turned her around and surveyed her from head to toe. "Beautiful," he said softly, his gaze catching and holding hers. "You take my breath away, Isabel."

She felt breathless, unable to pull even the tiniest bit of air into her lungs. He picked up her hand and placed it over the top button of his shirt. "I think I'm a bit overdressed, don't you?"

The thought of exposing all that hard, tanned flesh had her hands shaking as she worked on the first button. It slipped frustratingly out of her grasp.

"Relax." He captured her hand and lifted it to his mouth. "We're in no hurry here."

The calm, sexy assurance in his gaze grounded her, made her heart flip over in anticipation. Returning her fingers to the buttons, she managed to get the first one undone. Then the second and third, exposing a mouthwatering expanse of olive-skinned torso. *Dear heavens*, he had one of those six-packs, what looked like the consummate athlete's body. *Insane*.

She pushed the shirt off his shoulders, her mouth dry as she took him in. Alex groaned. "*Christós*, Izzie, touch me. I'm going a little nuts here...."

Emboldened by the want in his eyes, she lifted her hand to trace his pecs, feathering her palms down over his nipples. His quick intake of breath spurred her on, sending her hands down over the taut muscles of his washboard stomach. He was all hard male and nothing but. It thrilled and intimidated her at the same time.

Forcing herself not to think, she moved her hands to his belt, her unsteady but determined fingers pulling the leather from the buckle. His zipper was next, her hands brushing against his arousal as she pulled it down. He let out a tortured groan.

She lifted her gaze to his. "Should I stop?"

A harsh bark of laughter escaped him. "I would say that's the last thing you should do."

She kept going, unsure exactly about what she was supposed to be doing because with her ex there had never been any foreplay. Letting her instincts guide her, she slid her hands inside the waistband of his pants and pushed them down over his hips to the floor. He stepped out of them, clad only in a pair of sexy, body-hugging black boxers that did little to disguise the thick, hard length of him. At that moment, looking at his size, she wasn't at all sure this was going to work.

He must have seen the uncertainty in her face. Sliding his fingers under her jaw, he brought her gaze back up to his. "I'm big, Izzie, I know, but I promise I won't hurt you. We'll take this as slow as we need to, okay?"

She nodded, wondering why she trusted this man she hadn't even known for twenty-four hours more than she'd trusted anyone in her life. He lifted her up and carried her over to the huge king-size bed, the soft satin sheets and comforter of which were indeed white. Her head landed in the fluffy pillows, a smile curving her lips. "How's the hair?"

He ran his gaze lazily over her, his mouth quirking up on one side. "Better than I could have imagined."

Resting a knee on the bed, he looked every bit the part of an incredibly sexy Greek god, and her heart tripped over itself. Then went into freefall as he laid another one of those lazy, never-ending kisses on her that brought her body firing back to life in a heated rush. His hand slid down between her legs to caress her sensitized flesh, stroking her gently until she was once again writhing under his touch.

"Alex…" She wanted more this time. Wanted that incredible hard length of him she'd touched inside her.

He rose in a swift movement and stripped off his boxers, sheathing a condom over the jutting evidence of his arousal. She stared dry-mouthed at the size of his erection as he came back to her, his powerful thighs nudging hers apart. It had been two years since she'd been with her ex. Did your body go back to a virginal state after that amount of time? She supposed she was about to find out.

He read her expression easily. A corner of his mouth lifted in a teasing smile. "Sweetheart, you're so ready for me I can guarantee this isn't going to be an issue."

Her heart skipped a beat. And then his hands were sliding under her hips, lifting her as he moistened the tip of his erection with her wetness. Izzie closed her eyes, his erotic foreplay much too much for her to meet head-on.

The first couple of inches as he took her made her gasp and open her eyes. "Alex," she breathed, "I can't—"

"Shh." He set a finger against her lips, holding himself completely still. "Wait…"

She closed her eyes and tried to force herself to relax. And felt her body slowly loosen, stretch to accommodate him, until the discomfort she was feeling turned into something very different.

"Okay?"

She nodded her head up and down, opening her eyes. "More."

His gaze darkened, the iron control he was holding over himself evident in the tense set of his jaw as he slid another couple of inches into her. Pure pleasure sliced through her at the incredible feeling of him filling her, but still he held back. She arched her hips in invitation. "Alex," she murmured. "I'm good."

A muscle jumped in his jaw. "You sure?"

"Yes."

His thrust, as he took her completely, stole her breath. Had her digging her nails into the sheets at the feeling of him everywhere inside her, knowing she couldn't have taken another inch...another centimeter even.

He tightened his hands around her hips, withdrew ever so slowly, then eased into her again, making her feel it all over.

"*Theos*, Izzie, you feel so good," he gritted out, taking her again and again until she was half-crazy for him. Built a slow-burning fire he fanned with every rhythmic slide inside her.

"Wrap your legs around me," he encouraged huskily, her gasp of pleasure as she did so and felt him even deeper echoing throughout the room. And then there was no longer self-control, holding back. Now there was only his fierce, deep strokes as he buried himself inside her, his throaty words of encouragement as she took him deeper and deeper the most potent aphrodisiac. Her gaze met his as he slid his hands out from under her hips and braced them on either side of her, his muscular biceps holding him above her. Higher and higher, watching her the entire time, he took her ever closer to that insanely good release she now knew was right around the corner.

"Hell, Izzie," he ground out, a sheen of perspiration breaking out on his brow. "I can't stand this much longer."

She wrapped her legs tighter around his hips, her gaze locking onto his. "Now, Alex...I'm so close."

With a muttered curse, he drove into her then, faster, harder, until a burst of pleasure tightened her body around him and send her spiraling off into a wave of sensation that seemed to go on forever. He groaned as she contracted around him, swelled inside of her and found his own release, his hoarse cry the sexiest thing she thought she'd ever heard.

She lay there, his big body on top of her, limbs entangled with hers, their ragged breathing slowing on the night air. And knew that what had just happened was something incredibly unusual—that intense connection that had fueled everything between them today. She wasn't so naive she didn't realize that.

"Okay?" Alex lifted himself up on his forearms to study her face.

A smile she couldn't hide curved her lips. "More than okay."

"I'd have to agree with that," he said softly, shifting onto one arm so he could run a finger down her cheek. "That was incredible."

The heat that bloomed under his fingers must have been visible because he laughed softly and pulled her close. "A little late for shyness, *agape*. You blew me away."

Which was such a switch from what her ex had told her afterward. It was like wiping away the past in one fell, satisfying swoop. "The Greek is...very sexy," she murmured. "I think I'm a sucker for it."

He threw back his head and laughed. "I fall into it sometimes when I'm passionate about something." He brushed his thumb across her lower lip in a caress that gave her goose bumps, his voice deepening to a husky whisper. "I would demonstrate more but it's late and you look exhausted."

She *was* exhausted. And although she wanted to stay awake, to enjoy as much of this amazing night with Alex as she could, she didn't protest when he shifted onto his side and tucked her against his warm, hard frame. Exhaustion overtook her, settling her lashes down on her cheeks.

Her last thought was that this entire day had been meant to happen for a reason. She had been meant to face up to her biggest fear once and for all. Meant to enjoy this one amazing night with this incredible man. The problem was, she thought sleepily, she couldn't see any other man ever living up to it.

CHAPTER FIVE

"You're going to love me as usual."

Alex held his phone to his ear as he eased away from the warmth of Izzie's body and out of bed, his PA's comment making him smile. "I already love you for being up at—" he glanced at his watch as he walked out into the living room "—midnight working."

"You know I'm a control freak," she returned drily. "The plane and pilot are ready for you."

"You are amazing." He ran his fingers through his hair. "Remind me what the red tape is for flying someone else back on the jet...? Gerry just needs to add them to the manifest, right?"

"Yup. And they need their documentation." Papers rustled in the background. "Oh, and a producer from NYC-TV has been trying to get a hold of you. Is this something about the Messer case?"

He grimaced. "Yes. Tell them I'm in Maui."

"Is this going to turn into a circus?"

"Very possibly." But he was going to do his damnedest to shut Frank Messer down before it got to that. "Get some sleep. Come in a bit later if you like."

She yawned. "As if, with the amount of work on my plate. See you tomorrow."

He stepped into the shower while Izzie slept, letting the

hot sting of the spray ease the tension in his shoulders. As amazing as last night had been, it now seemed like an ill-advised foray into a complication he didn't need. Every second he spent doing anything other than figuring out how to beat Frank Messer was time he couldn't afford to lose. He needed to get back to New York, meet with his lawyers and put together a game plan.

He did not need the distraction of Izzie on a transatlantic flight with him. The odds of him keeping his hands off of her were slim to none, and that just couldn't happen. Last night had been an agreed-upon one-night stand. An opportunity to enjoy each other as two consenting adults.

Also unbelievably hot... The look on Izzie's face when she'd come apart in his arms on the terrace made his body stir to life under the pounding, hot spray. The extreme pleasure of driving into that tight, welcoming warmth of hers a seriously tempting invitation to put his pilot off a half hour longer and wake her up. But he needed to get out of here, Izzie needed to sleep and she already had a flight booked. The better idea would be to send a car for her and get out.

He shut off the shower, dried himself and slung a towel around his hips. It was better for both of them to end it now. Clean. Neat.

He headed into the bedroom and pulled on a pair of boxers and a T-shirt.

"What time is it?"

A still half-asleep Izzie sat up and rubbed her eyes. A gorgeous Izzie, he might add, her long dark hair falling over her edible shoulders as she struggled to focus. His gaze dropped to her pink-tipped, perfectly shaped breasts where the sheet had slipped and he got hard all over again.

She flushed and dragged the sheet up to her collarbone. "It feels early."

"It's five-thirty," he said briefly, pulling on a pair of

jeans. "I have to go, but you should sleep. I'll send a car for 8:30 to take you to the airport…"

She pushed her hair back, a confused look spreading across her face. "I—er, aren't we on the same flight?"

He walked over and sat down beside her on the bed. "The jet's been fixed. I need to get out of here."

"Oh." The wounded look in her eyes made him feel like a total cad.

"I have an emergency to take care of," he explained, unable to stop himself from sliding a hand under the sheet and cupping one of her gorgeous breasts, the tip hardening immediately under the caress of his thumb. He watched her eyes darken to that same chocolate-brown, almost-black color they had last night when he'd made love to her. "It's better you rest and take the later flight."

She nodded, but the slight wobble in her chin near killed him. He bent his head and brushed his lips over hers. "Thank you for last night."

But what was meant to serve as a brief kiss that would have secured him an appropriate exit was quickly revealed for the mistake it was, her mouth softening and parting underneath his, the attraction that was electric between them sparking to life. He groaned, unable to help himself from enjoying one more taste of her, it had just been so incredibly sweet last night. Tunneling his hands in her hair, he took the kiss deeper until she curled her hands in his T-shirt and this was only going in one direction…

He pulled back before he lost his head completely. "I have to go."

Her teeth sank into her bottom lip and she nodded. Brushing a chunk of her thick hair out of her face, he tucked it behind her ear. "I left some clothes for you on the chair. They're too big for you, but they're clean."

"Thanks."

He held her gaze, refusing to issue false promises. "Keep jumping, Iz. It's the only way to live."

She said nothing, those big eyes on him. He finished dressing and grabbed his wallet and watch before he changed his mind. It wasn't until he was halfway through the door that he stopped and turned around.

"No regrets?"

A wry smile curved her mouth. "No regrets."

"Good." He turned around and made himself leave, wondering why it was so hard to walk away. He'd done it a million times. This time felt different.

Izzie took a deep breath as she heard the front door of the penthouse click shut. Took another, tried to calm herself, and when that didn't work, picked up the nearest missile, which happened to be Alex's pillow, and chucked it against the wall, pretending it was him. Had he actually just left her here like that? When he knew she needed to get back to New York? *Really*? She sank back against the pillows, her breath coming out in a long *whoosh.* How hard would it have been for him to wait? He could have woken her up and she'd have been ready in five minutes flat, much happier to go with him now than wait for her flight.

Unbelievable. She stared at the pink dawn creeping across the London sky through the floor-to-ceiling windows. She'd just been unceremoniously dropped like a hot potato by a man who couldn't seem to get out of here fast enough. As if he'd thought she'd make a scene.

Scowling, she hugged her arms around herself. Maybe some of his women did that. But not her. She'd said one night and she'd meant one night. The last thing she needed to do was complicate her life right now. Not when she had a seven-hour flight and a panel of network executives to face on the other end of it, if James did indeed manage to persuade them to stay.

Not when she'd promised herself she'd never let a man rule her emotions the way her mother had her father's.

But heavens, it'd been worth it. The image of Alex on a dartboard faded to one of him naked on this bed, his beautiful body giving her more pleasure than she'd ever dreamed possible. Warmth flooded her cheeks. How she'd let him do those things to her on the terrace in full view of anyone who'd have cared to look… His husky encouragements to tell him what she wanted releasing a completely wanton side of her she hadn't even known existed…*God.* That *I'd be incredible in bed* tattoo he wore across his chest? Definitely not false advertising.

She threw the covers off, swung her legs over the side of the bed and headed for the shower. There was no way she was going to be able to go back to sleep after that last kiss, which had made her want to turn her one-night plan into a whole lot more. But since he had now *dumped* her, that wouldn't be a problem.

She pulled on the huge Boston College athletics T-shirt he'd left her, obviously his, and the pair of jeans that necessitated three roll-ups so she didn't trip over them. It wasn't fashionable, but it was necessary with her suitcase in New York without her.

Padding her way into the kitchen, she told herself she was going to be the smart girl she was and relegate Alex to her good—make that hot—memory book. The thing that had made her realize how completely she hadn't been living her life.

Mouth firm, she settled down on a kitchen bar stool with a cup of coffee she managed to wring out of the high-tech espresso machine, and went over the interview questions James had sent. She was going to give this interview her best shot. Forget about the past, know she'd worked hard and had grown so much, and put her demons aside.

This was the new Izzie. Time to unleash her on the world.

Sixteen hours later, Izzie exited her interview with the network execs in NYC-TV's Rockefeller Plaza offices so physically and mentally exhausted she could hardly put one foot in front of the other. A transatlantic flight, a whirlwind cab trip to the studios, and an hour and a half of nonstop grilling by the execs could do that to a person.

Visions of a bergamot-scented bath filled her head. She tucked her portfolio under her arm and stumbled her way through the newsroom, ignoring the envious, almost spiteful, look on Katy Phillip's face as she passed the entertainment desk. *So not going there.* She'd had a lot of that since she'd walked in this afternoon as the emerging star and she didn't have the strength to process it.

She sat down at her desk, thankful she hadn't been out on assignment today, with a story to edit ahead of her. Tomorrow was soon enough to catch up on email and everything else waiting for her. She yanked off her pumps, pulled her sneakers out of her bottom drawer and had just about laced them up when her boss's shiny loafers appeared in front of her.

Damn. She'd been so close...

"I heard it went well."

"I think so." She finished tying her sneaker and straightened up. "Given I was pretty much comatose."

James plopped down on the corner of her desk and crossed his arms over his chest. "They loved you. They think you have the young, fresh look that will appeal to the demographic we're going after."

She grinned. "Really?"

"Really." His face lit up. "They think you're very talented."

Her stomach muscles relaxed, a wave of relief flooding through her. "And the bad?"

"They're worried you're not experienced enough to handle the pressure."

Go figure. So was *she*.

"I told them any daughter of Dayla St. James is more than up to it."

Her mouth dropped open, dismay spreading through her. "What did you do that for?"

He scowled. "We're in it to win it, Iz. Get with the program."

The program didn't include her mother. *Ever.* "James, you know I want to do this on my own."

He waved a hand at her. "You want to make it in this business, you use the weapons at your disposal. This is a once-in-a-lifetime shot. Nobody's going to play nice."

She nodded. "I know that, I do. And I appreciate the opportunity. I'd just rather keep her out of it."

"You know that's never going to happen."

It would if she had anything to do with it. "What next, then?"

"They're putting together a short list. I'm pretty sure you'll be on it. Then they'll do trial weekends with each of the candidates. Meanwhile," he said, dumping a file on her desk, "we amp up your star potential with the Constantinou story. This," he said, pointing to the file, "is the real reason I want this interview."

She frowned. "I thought it was the juicy court case."

"That's good stuff." He flipped the file open and pointed at a magazine cover. "This is better."

She looked down at the glossy sports magazine. Squinted at the photo of the lone figure dressed in a football uniform, kneeling on a dusty field, helmet in hand. Felt the blood drain from her face. It couldn't be…. There was just no way. Her gaze flew to the headline. The Next King of Football? Is College Quarterback Sensation Alexios Constantinou the Player Who Will Revive Pro Football in New York?

Her head spun; the lights of the busy newsroom blurred around her. The football player in the photo was undoubtedly Alex, the man she'd just spent the night with.

"I thought his name was *Leandros*," she croaked.

"Goes by his middle name," James dismissed. "Something about his father disowning him."

Oh my God. Alex was Alexios. Alexios Constantinou. *Who'd supposedly been long gone by the time she'd gotten to Sophoros's London offices*, according to his receptionist. Her mind flashed back to the blonde's expression when she'd asked how long *Leandro* had been gone. The challenging look on the receptionist's face. *She'd been right.* She'd had Leandros Constantinou, *Alex,* under her fingertips the entire time. Had been stuck in an elevator with him for hours…and what had she done? She'd *slept with him.*

OMG.

"Izzie?"

Her boss was staring at her. She shook her head, trying desperately to contain her horror. "Why does it matter that he was a football player? This is about Frank Messer's offer to tell all."

James settled himself more comfortably on her desk. "Alexios Constantinou was one of the best quarterbacks to ever come out of the college system. Charismatic, smart, he was a born leader…a real golden boy. Led his team to a national championship and was drafted first overall by the New York Crusaders. He was touted as the player who would put football back on the map in the Big Apple. The problem is—" her boss grimaced "—we can't leave a player like that alone in this city. We have to pile the pressure on him until he cracks and we have a self-fulfilling prophecy."

Her gaze slid to the photo, her brain still trying to catch up. Alex had been a star football player?

"So what happened?" she asked warily.

"The press was all over him like he was the second coming. Expected him to turn the team around way too fast." His mouth twisted. "He almost did it, too, in his third year. Then he blew his rotator cuff in a qualifying game for the playoffs and ended his career for good. Twenty-four years old and his career was over. One of the true tragic stories in professional sports."

Her stomach twisted in a sea of knots. *Sometimes in life you're only given one shot,* Alex had said in the elevator. *Use it wisely.*

She cleared her throat. "Okay, so all very dramatic, but isn't it ancient history now? And what does this have to do with Frank Messer?"

An intense, self-satisfied smile curved her boss's lips. "The night Alex Constantinou was injured, he disappeared, never did another interview. Then he resurfaces a few years later with this red-hot software company he's created with his college buddy and they launch this title, *Behemoth*, that sets the gaming world on fire. The man's probably made a hundred times more money on it than he would ever have made in football, but he still never talks to media. Ever." His gaze locked on hers. "I want that story. *His* story."

Her brain whirled, tried to keep up. "So you want to land the exclusive story on Alexios Constantinou and use Frank Messer as leverage."

"Exactly. And you'll be the one to convince him. Everyone knows Constantinou has an eye for the ladies."

Izzie almost choked on that. *Dear Lord.* She waved her hand at him. "If he hates the press that much, James, he isn't going to do it. He'll say to hell with public opinion and let the courts decide."

Her boss shrugged. "I think we can convince him it's better to tell his side of the story than let Messer do it for him."

"*If* the lawyers let him...."

He lifted a brow. "CEOs are mavericks. Especially this guy. He'll do what he wants. You just need to convince him."

Right. Her stomach lurched. What would Alex think of her when he realized what she did for a living? It wasn't as if she'd deliberately tried to mislead him about her profession. After a few nasty encounters with people who weren't fans of the media, including a guy who'd verbally assaulted her in a bar, she didn't advertise what she did upon first meeting. It just made life easier to say she was in communications.

Until now.

Every muscle in her body screamed out that she couldn't do this. But how was she supposed to tell her boss that? And *why*.

James looked at her expectantly. "Well?"

Her brain spit out a desperate solution. She'd find a way to discredit Messer so the story never became an issue. So they had nothing to strong-arm Alex with. Her boss could find her another juicy assignment that *didn't* involve the man she'd just devoured last night and everyone would be happy.

"Okay," she said, nodding. "I'll call Messer in the morning and schedule a background interview."

He nodded. "And *find* Constantinou. He's back in the country. I don't care if you have to camp out in front of his office building."

She was so never doing that. James slid off her desk and did his usual pre-news-hour circuit of the room. Izzie shoved her phone in her purse and stared at the lucky silver charm dangling from the strap. How could this have happened to her? Of all the men she could have chosen to have a one-night stand with, it had to have been *Alexios Constantinou*?

Inconceivable. She stood up, deciding she'd do a better job figuring this out in the bathtub. A commotion near the entrance to the newsroom made her look up. A petite brunette stood court in the middle of a group of reporters, her megawatt smile on full display. *Her mother.* Good Lord. She was back in town.

Dayla St. James chatted for a few minutes with the crowd, reveling in the attention they heaped on her, then blew them a kiss and made her way over to Izzie's desk with that same shoulders-back, confident strut she'd been using her entire life. Izzie blew out a long breath and steeled herself for the hurricane that was her mother.

"I'm back," Dayla announced unnecessarily, arriving in a flurry of floral perfume to press a kiss to both of Izzie's cheeks. Her mother's violet eyes took her in, the heart-shaped face that had sent a billion men's hearts fluttering still so absolutely perfect at fifty-one she made Izzie feel like an awkward, overblown offshoot. "I've come to whisk you off for a drink."

Izzie sat down on the edge of her desk. She needed to process, not go for a drink. This was what little white lies were for. "I have plans with the girls."

Her mother frowned. "Surely you can have a quick drink with me first? I'm going to get all tangled up in this play tomorrow and I haven't seen you in weeks."

She groaned inwardly. "How long is your engagement?"

"Three months," her mother said with satisfaction. "Perfect timing for me to help you with your anchor run."

Izzie stared at her. "How could you possibly know about that already? *I* just found out."

"The network is one big gossip machine, Iz. You know that."

She hadn't thought it worked *that* fast. She sighed. "Look, Mother, we both know what happened last time you tried to give me advice. I need to do this on my own."

Her mother's ultrasharp gaze softened. "Izzie, you were so young. I never should have pushed you into that audition. You weren't ready."

No kidding. She winced, remembering that stiflingly hot day in L.A. as if it were yesterday. Her mother had pulled strings to get her a trial for an entertainment reporter position with a national news show at the network she'd been doing a television sitcom for at the time. Fresh out of school and nervous as hell, Izzie had been up against competition with five times her experience, and known the only reason she was in the room was because the producer was half in love with her mother.

"It was a disaster," Izzie muttered. "I completely fell apart."

"You were terrified. It was wrong of me to do that."

Had it been? Or had she just choked? Izzie cringed, remembering how she'd forgotten first one line, then another, her mother's face getting redder and redder as her daughter blew it over and over again. Until finally the producer, a sympathetic look on his face, had suggested that they call it a day.

Her jaw tightened as she remembered how silent her mother had been on the drive home. As if to say, *I knew you were the ordinary, less spectacular daughter, but did you have to embarrass me that badly?*

She wrapped her arms around herself. "I've made my way here, Mother. My career has been all me. You need to respect that."

Her mother nodded. "I respect the fact that you want to do this on your own. In fact," she lifted a brow, "I applaud that. But you need to start letting me in. I've been trying for months to make things right between us and all you keep doing is pushing me away."

Izzie gave her mother a disbelieving look as Dayla delivered the line as though she was on a set with a live audience of hundreds. How could she think a few months of sporadic attempts to connect with her daughter was going to make up for a lifetime of not caring? "You need to earn that right, Mother."

"I'm trying to. But you aren't budging an inch."

Izzie's mouth flattened. "Unlike you, I'm not good at command performances."

Her mother's frown deepened. Izzie watched her mentally check herself and pull her mouth out of its twist. Frowns were bad for business. Frowns took years off your career. "Sometimes I think you're the one who has the drama degree, Izzie."

She got pointedly to her feet. "How about Wednesday for dinner?"

Her mother nodded, halfway across the room before she tossed her parting barb. "I'll have Clara make reservations for sushi. We have to keep you in anchor shape."

Oh my God. Izzie balled her hands into fists. "I hate sushi!"

"Oh that's right…" Her mother disappeared through the double glass doors leaving devastation behind in her wake. As usual.

Izzie picked up her phone and called Jo, deciding a bottle of wine at her best friend's place superseded the need for a bath. She tossed the Messer file into her bag; she'd read it on the subway ride over to Jo's. There had to be *something* in that file that would discredit Frank Messer. Because interviewing Alex was not an option. Ever.

CHAPTER SIX

"YOU NEED TO stop looking like you're being dragged to your execution," Jo chided, pushing Izzie through the tuxedo- and ball gown-clad crowd toward the bar. "It's just an interview. Ask him to do it and get it over with."

"Easy for you to say," Izzie muttered. "You're not the one who told a half truth, then had a ridiculously hot one-night stand with the man you're supposed to be interviewing."

"Oh come on, Iz." Jo slid onto a stool at the gleaming ebony bar and lifted a brow at her. "How many scrapes did we get ourselves out of in J school? Where is your adventurous spirit?"

"This is not creative ways to explain covering a high-end escort service as our final project," Izzie retorted, sliding onto the stool beside her. "Why couldn't you have lectured me *after* Italy?"

"Then you wouldn't have had the big night with the stud." Jo's smile was ear to ear. "Which was the best thing that's ever happened to you, by the way."

Izzie made a face at her. The bartender came over, leaned his palms on the rich dark wood and gave Jo a long look. "What'll you have?"

"Two dirty martinis," Jo said with a flirtatious smile. "Heavy on the olives."

"You got it." He gave her friend one last admiring look before grabbing a shaker.

Izzie groaned. "You are something else. It's like every man in the world is programmed to love you."

Jo lifted a brow. "I send out pheromones, Iz. *Phare-o-moans*. As in I give guys a chance. You're so caught up in your 'up at six for a run, eight to eight caffeine-induced endurance race' you wouldn't know fun if it hit you in the butt."

Izzie glared at her. "That is so unfair. I have a career. I'm climbing the ladder…"

"You need some fun in your life. Desperately."

"I *do* have fun."

"You think putting purple nail polish on your toes is a walk on the wild side. I'm talking *fun*."

"Yes, well, look where all the wildness has gotten me." She'd spent the last two days trying to discredit Frank Messer in a desperate attempt *not* to do this, but the more she'd spoken with him and researched, the more credible he'd become. He'd played an awfully significant role in the creation of *Behemoth* and everyone in the industry knew it. So here she was, stuck in the vomit-inducing position of having to approach Alex at this gala event for the Met that NYC-TV was sponsoring, to ask him for the interview.

The gala was hosted in the museum's breathtaking Temple of Dendur with its exotic ambient lighting and ancient temples lit by a mystical, otherworldly glow, and the organizers had perfectly captured the spirit and ambience of ancient Egyptian times. But instead of enjoying the atmosphere, Izzie had spent the whole evening searching for Alex's tall, dark figure, her heart in her mouth.

She'd twisted back around on her stool to watch Jo bestow another high-wattage smile on the flirtatious bartender, when her friend's eyes sharpened on the crowd. "Tall, black hair, blue eyes, you said?"

Izzie froze, a fist tightening in her chest. "Yes, why, do you see him?"

"Killer body?"

"Yes," she croaked, her throat dry as the Sahara.

"This could be him. He's with another guy—blond, nerdy in a cute kinda way."

"His business partner, Mark," Izzie said weakly. She'd done her research.

A low whistle escaped her friend. "Wow, Iz. He is *smoking.*"

Not helping. The crowded room seemed to close in on her as she turned ever so slowly and followed Jo's gaze. Suddenly it was terribly, impossibly hard to breathe. Alex was standing talking to the Met's PR person, not fifty feet away, the black Armani tux he wore drool-inducing on his tall, powerful frame.

She whipped her head around before he could see her, pressed clammy hands against her thighs. What was she supposed to do now? Walk up to him, say hi and unload her bombshell? She'd spent so much time trying to discredit Messer she didn't have a plan. And suddenly that seemed very stupid indeed.

"Drink," Jo said, shoving the martini at her. "A bit of liquid courage is all you need."

Alex smiled at whatever the PR woman for the Met was saying, hearing none of it. He detested the inane small talk these occasions required. Yes, she was glad Sophoros had sponsored the evening. Yes, he understood his checkbook was important to the organization's continued success. He got it. Enough.

He was tired. His temper was short. Pretty much bottom of the barrel since his lawyers had told him Frank Messer was going to be a big, huge pain in his behind. He needed to figure a way out of this mess with the least damage to Sophoros and he wasn't doing that here making small talk.

The PR person finally took the hint and moved on to

schmooze another of the sponsors. Alex shot a glance at Mark. "Ready to get out of here?"

His partner nodded. "Except you might want to check out the blonde at the bar near the fountain. She's been staring at you for a few minutes now and she's a looker."

Normally all about the blondes, Alex found himself bored by the thought. He'd been annoyingly, persistently consumed by thoughts of a particular voluptuous brunette all week. And even though he'd told himself Izzie was all wrong for him, that he didn't need a woman distracting him when being on his game was all that mattered, he couldn't get her out of his head.

Hell. He glanced in the direction Mark was looking. His partner was right. The blonde *was* stunning. The kind of leggy, sophisticated beauty he'd normally be all over. And she *was* staring at him. But it was the brunette beside her who caught his eye. Her back to him, she had the same long, thick chestnut hair and curvaceous body Izzie had. And the dress she had on was fantastic, a body-hugging number that left her back completely bare...

"Something else, isn't she?" Mark muttered.

"So is the woman beside her." His gaze sharpened on the brunette. Something in the way she held herself, in the tilt of her head, reminded him of Izzie. And now he was losing his mind, because in a city of eight million, the chances of Izzie being here were slim to none.

He was just about to turn away when the brunette twisted slightly in her seat to look at them. He stiffened, his gaze locking onto her face. *It was Izzie.* Minus the dark-rimmed glasses he'd removed before taking her to bed. He took in how the gown molded her delectable figure, her wide-eyed stare as she sat frozen on the stool. And wondered how fate had put her in his path twice in one week.

His gaze narrowed as she slid off the stool and walked quickly toward the opposite end of the ballroom. *She was running away from him?* He stared incredulously as she hightailed it through the crowd as fast as those ridiculously high shoes she was wearing allowed.

"I'll be right back," he muttered to Mark, clenching his teeth. Women didn't walk away from him. And certainly not this one.

Izzie knew the minute Alex started to follow her. It was like a centrifugal force that pulled on her steps, threatened to drag her back toward him, but she kept going, determined to face him when she had her wits about her. And that was not now.

She twisted her way through the crowd, as fast as she could go in her prize possession four-inch designer heels. Trained her gaze on the ladies' room doors.

"Izzie." It was a command, not an address. She kept walking. She was almost there, just a few more steps and—

"Izzie." Alex clamped a hand down on her shoulder and swung her around. "What are you doing?"

She swallowed hard, her high heels bringing her face-to-face with his furious glare. "I—I needed to use the ladies' room."

"At the exact moment you saw me?" The scathing disbelief in his voice made her cringe. "Try again."

Heat filled her cheeks. She shifted her weight to the other foot, her gaze dropping away from his. "Believe what you like. I need to pee."

The look on his face told her he didn't believe her for a second. But he dropped his hand and took a step back. "Fine. I'll be here." He propped himself up against the wall near the entrance to the ladies' room, arms crossed over his chest. Izzie lowered her gaze and stalked past him.

She took an extraordinarily long time while she collected herself. Debated how to approach what she had to do. When she came out, he was standing in exactly the

same place, arms crossed over his chest, looking indo-
lently, indecently gorgeous. She made an attempt at casual, but a lacing of bitterness edged her voice. "How was
your flight?"

His dark brows drew together. "I had to leave, Izzie. I
told you I had an emergency."

Frank Messer. She reminded herself what this night
was all about. Business. Not acting like a girl. She waved
a hand at him. "It's fine. I'm over it."

"Then why walk away like that?"

She shook her head. "I told you I—"

"Needed to use the washroom." He gave her a grim
look. "Okay, let's try this another way." Taking her arm,
he walked her toward the exit. Her pulse accelerated at the
thought of being alone with him again and that was just
silly, because what she should be focusing on was convinc-
ing him to do this interview.

"That was your friend Jo, I assume." He stood back
while she preceded him through the French doors to the
outdoor terrace, deserted except for a couple of men smoking. "She looks like a man slayer."

"The poor bartender was drooling all over her."

"She's attractive."

Izzie blinked at the understatement. "You don't think
she's gorgeous?"

"I think *you're* gorgeous." He stopped at the far end of
the terrace that overlooked the gardens and leaned back
against the wall that separated the two, his gaze moving
over her in a leisurely inspection that lingered on every
curve.

"Alex," she muttered. "Stop looking at me like that."

"Why should I when you look so sensational in that
dress?" A mocking glint entered his eyes. "When I saw
you I thought it couldn't be you—it's such a crazy coincidence that we'd both be here."

Her cheeks heated to boiling. *Tell him now, Izzie.*

He shrugged his broad shoulders. "Then I convinced myself I must have conjured you up. I've been thinking about you, Iz. A lot…"

The world came to a grinding halt. "You have?"

"Mmm." He nodded. "I was wondering how you made out in the interview."

Oh. Her heart dropped. Of course he hadn't *really* been thinking about her.

"Izzie." His low, husky laughter wrapped itself around her. "I'm teasing you."

He stepped in close, picked up her hand and brought it to his lips, pressing an openmouthed kiss to her palm. "What are you doing?" she asked in a strangled tone.

"Checking to see if you taste as good as I remember."

Oh, God. "Alex, I—

"Ssh—" He lifted his lips from her hand and pressed his thumb against her mouth.

Her stomach did a loop-to-loop. A wry smile curved his lips. "As hard as I try not to, all I keep thinking about is you in my bed, Iz…"

His deep, velvet tone made her heart race. Her lower lip trembled as his thumb dropped away from her mouth and he bent his head to hers. "Have you?"

"Have I what?" she asked helplessly.

"Have you thought about me?"

One last shred of self-preservation kicked in as she remembered how he'd left her in London. "I thought we agreed it was only one night."

"Does it *feel* like it's over?" he growled, dragging her closer so she could feel his heart pounding against hers.

No. No, it didn't. She braced herself as he brought his mouth firmly down on hers, staking his claim. A wild flurry of excitement at being in his arms again rushed through her. With a helpless sigh, she wound her arms around his neck and kissed him back. Just one kiss…

"I like this dress," he muttered against her lips, his hands burning into her bare skin as he swept them down her back. "Hell, Izzie, I have no self-control when it comes to you."

His words thrilled her, sent a shiver of excitement down her spine. She lost herself in the feeling of his hands on her again. The sensuous slant of his mouth as he nudged hers open and took the kiss deeper. She arched her neck, welcoming the sweep of his tongue as it slid against hers. He groaned and dragged her against the hard length of his body. Started an ache deep inside her she wanted desperately to assuage the same way they had the last time.

"Come home with me," he urged raggedly.

Her body said yes. But her brain… She yanked herself out of his arms and took an unsteady step backward. Sucked in a breath. "I have something I need to tell you…"

He frowned, running a distracted hand through his hair as his gaze tracked her. "Okay…"

She swallowed hard. "When I told you that night in London I was in communications I didn't tell you the—"

"There you two are."

She looked up, horrified, as James walked across the terrace toward them, his eyes glittering with the satisfaction of a hunter who'd cornered his prey. "You're a hard man to find, Constantinou."

Alex drew his brows together. "Do I know you?"

James stopped in front of him, sticking out his hand. "Izzie's boss, James Curry, from NYC-TV."

Alex froze. Kept his hands by his sides. "The James Curry who's been calling my office every day for a week?"

"The very same," her boss acknowledged, unperturbed. "Has Izzie gotten around to explaining what we want to do with the exclusive?"

Alex's voice was icy cold as he turned to her. "You're a reporter."

Izzie blanched, every ounce of blood in her body seeming to flee to her feet. "I was just about to explain."

Her boss's gaze swung to Izzie, then back to Alex. "Do you two know each other?"

Alex's mouth tightened. "Nice try, Curry. Wasn't half a dozen unreturned phone calls enough to convince you I'm not interested?"

Her boss shrugged. "Messer's going to kill you in the court of public opinion."

"Messer doesn't have a leg to stand on."

James lifted his shoulders. "Do you really want to take a chance on that?"

Alex's gaze flicked to Izzie, moving scathingly over her. "So you sent Isabel to *persuade* me? Don't you think that's going a bit far?"

"I thought some female persuasion might help, yes."

Izzie felt herself sink into the depths of hell. "James," she interjected, "why don't you let Alex and I finish our conversation? We can—"

"Actually," Alex interrupted, "I'd like to know...do you often ask your reporters to go to the lengths Izzie did for this story? Or was I a special case?"

Her boss frowned. "I have no idea what you're talking about."

Alex's fists clenched by his sides. "You really are scum of the earth, aren't you?" He took a step closer to James, his six-feet-plus, wide-shouldered frame dwarfing her boss's slighter one. James stood toe to toe with him, unfazed, his chin jutting out belligerently.

"What are you talk—"

"*James.*" Izzie stepped between the two men, heart pounding. "Please go inside. I'll handle this."

Her boss shook his head. "I don't think I should—"

"That's an excellent suggestion, Curry," Alex broke in, a dangerous glimmer lighting his eyes. "Why don't you follow it before I do what my fists are itching to do."

Her boss looked from Alex to Izzie and back. "I think you should ex—"

"James," Izzie broke in desperately. "Alex and I have something we need to discuss. Please go. I'll find you afterward."

Her boss gave her an uncertain look. Izzie pleaded with him with her eyes. "All right," he said finally. "Think about it, Constantinou. It's the smart thing to do."

Izzie watched him go, sucking in a deep breath. Alex looked her over, his voice so cold, it sent a shiver down her spine. "You should have been an actress like your mother," he drawled. "Your performance was utterly brilliant, Iz. I bought the naive young thing hook, line and sinker."

She shook her head. "It isn't anything like that. I was coming to track you down that day, yes, but I had no idea who you were when we got stuck in that elevator. Your receptionist said you'd left hours earlier and I was looking for Leandros, not Alex."

His lip curled. "You expect me to believe that? You forget I have a hell of a lot of experience dealing with the media. I know exactly what lengths reporters will go to for a story, although I have to admit prostituting yourself is above and beyond."

"Prostituting myself?" She stared at him, horrified. "I would never do that, Alex, I—"

"How did you manage it?" A disdainful glitter shone in his eyes. "My schedule was all over the place that day."

She shook her head, knowing this was getting way out of control. "I didn't manage anything. I went into reception, asked for *Leandros*, they told me you had gone back to the U.S. and I left. You were very closemouthed about yourself that night."

"You wonder why," he came back savagely. "So you just *happened* to get stuck in that elevator with me. Are you even afraid of them by the way?"

"Yes." She took a deep breath. "Alex, be reasonable here."

"Given what's going on in my head, I think I'm being exceedingly reasonable."

He *looked* like he wanted to put his hands around her neck and strangle her. She took a step backward. "I swear to you I had no idea who you were until I came back to work and James showed me a picture of you. Everything that happened between us was real."

"You expect me to believe *that*?" His blue eyes gleamed with leashed fury. "How much of a fool do you think I am?"

"You heard James," she said desperately. "He had no idea what you were talking about. This wasn't a setup, it was—"

"Enough." He ground the word out with such force she stopped in her tracks. She backed up until she met the hard concrete of the wall. He followed her, pinning her against it. "No more lies."

She willed herself not to flinch as he took her jaw in his hand. "What if I'd been an overweight, unattractive has-been, Iz? Would you still have had the guts to seduce me?"

She raised her chin in defiance. "I went to bed with you for exactly the reasons I told you in London."

Disbelief flared in his eyes. "What was that—oh yes, I remember now," he jeered, his gaze raking over her. "You didn't want to have any regrets. For once in your life you wanted to go after what you wanted. Well, you sure did, Iz. Too bad it was a wasted effort."

Tears stung the back of her eyes. How dare he dismantle their wildly romantic night and make it into something dirty and disgraceful. "It wasn't—"

"Tell me something, Iz." He slid his thumb across her trembling lower lip. "Did you enjoy yourself while you did your duty? Or were those little moans all an act?"

She lifted her hand to slap him, but he caught it easily in his own before she got it halfway to his face. "Save it," he bit out grimly. "I've had enough."

He took a step back, his face hard as stone. "Tell your boss he has a snowball's chance in hell of getting this story." Then he turned and strode back inside, his long, furious steps eating up the length of the terrace. She stared blindly at the entrance, at the lights and laughter of a party still in full swing. Sank back against the wall, palms sweaty, heart racing. How had it all gone so horribly wrong? How could she have predicted Alex would drag her out here and kiss her after walking out on her in London? That he would want a repeat performance of that night as much as she did?

She pressed her fingers to her lips, still stinging from the intensity of his kiss. A kiss that had thrown her off her game completely...made her believe they might have something together. *Stupid*, she berated herself. Stupid, stupid, stupid. How could she have made such a mess of this? How could Alex think she had set him up like that? *Slept with him to get an interview?* It was inconceivable.

A wave of perspiration broke out on her brow. How was she going to convince Alex it had all been a huge, crazy coincidence?

What was she going to tell her boss?

She found him inside, talking to a producer from a rival station. He blew off the conversation and cornered her in a quiet spot behind the exhibits. "What is going on, Izzie?"

She took a deep breath and squared her shoulders. "I will fix this, James."

"You sure as hell will. What in God's name was Constantinou talking about? What setup?"

Her stomach lurched. "It's complicated. He's just…misinterpreted something."

His gaze narrowed. "Misinterpreted what?"

She pressed her lips together. "This has nothing to do with work, James, we—I— It's personal."

"I can see that. When were you going to tell me you knew him?"

"He's just an acquaintance. He's misunderstood something. Give me a chance to make this right and I will."

Her boss sighed. Seemed to run out of anger. "Look, Izzie, I know you wouldn't do anything unethical. It's just not you. So whatever's going on…fix it and get that interview."

She nodded. That's exactly what she was going to do. She just had no idea *how* she was going to do it. What exactly did the odds of a "snowball's chance in hell" equate to?

CHAPTER SEVEN

ALEX COULD COUNT on one hand the times in his life he'd made a decision that went against his instincts. It had made him difficult to coach on the football field. He'd been dubbed the Rebel Quarterback for his penchant for changing a play late in the game, giving his coaches a virtual heart attack. But nine times out of ten he'd won the game. Because his instincts, his feel for the field, had always been dead-on.

But standing here, looking out at the Manhattan skyline from Sophoros's fiftieth-floor offices, he was about to act against them. After an epic battle between him and the PR team, he had conceded they had to be proactive about the way the Messer case was framed in the media. The interview with NYC-TV, his director of PR had insisted, was the perfect contained opportunity to do so. Isabel Peters was anything but a hard-edged reporter, they could play it as they liked, and the network would syndicate it across the country, allowing him then to go underground, his version of the story out there.

He blew out a long breath and pressed a hand against the glass. Laura Reed was one of the best PR people in the country. The lawyers were okay with the strategy, with certain ground rules. It was the right thing to do. Except every bone in his body was telling him not to do it. He'd spent eight years avoiding the media. Eight years avoiding any chance that some fame-seeking reporter would smell something wrong about the night his career had ended and expose his biggest mistake. And *now* he was going to jeopardize that?

His stomach twisted, contracted as though it was being put through a sieve. Laura Reed had called this a contained story. There was only one person on the planet who knew about his biggest lapse in judgment, and that person would never talk. He had to do this. Had to contain Frank Messer in the only way possible. But to give the interview to Izzie after she'd deceived him like that? It made his soul burn.

He slammed his palm against the glass. That he'd fallen into James Curry's trap so easily was downright embarrassing. How had his radar not picked up on what Izzie was? Because of course she'd been staking him out. He'd deliberately waited until the crowds were gone to get on that elevator, and she'd stood there jabbering on her phone until exactly the right moment to jump on with him.

What he wanted to know was why she hadn't asked him about the interview that night in London while she'd had the chance. Why had she waited until the charity event to ambush him? Had she been trying to soften him up first? Then make the ask?

He rubbed his hand over his face, fatigue attacking every cell of his body. If he were to be honest, the disappointment was the worst. Yes, he'd lusted after her that night as any red-blooded male would have. But it had been more than that. He'd liked Izzie. She'd seemed different from the jaded, ambitious women who filled his social circles. And when he'd seen her again that night, he couldn't stay away. Hadn't wanted to.

His mouth tightened as he looked down at the midday

traffic jamming Lexington Avenue. He'd broken his iron-clad rule not to trust another female after one night of potently good sex. Crazy, when there couldn't be a man alive who'd received such a clear demonstration of the untrustworthiness of women than him, not once but twice in his life. First with his mother, who'd walked out on his family for another man. Then with his own blind faith in the fiancée he'd been so madly in love with he hadn't seen her betrayal coming until she'd set her engagement ring down on the kitchen table and told him she was leaving him for his biggest competition—the man who'd taken his job and his dream along with it.

He would never trust a woman again. *Ever*. So why had Izzie gotten to him so?

Why did he *still* want her?

He let out a curse and levered himself away from the window. Even after everything she'd done, he still burned for her. Maybe it was the desire for revenge…maybe he just couldn't get enough. Whatever it was, it was still insistently *there*.

He walked to his desk and picked up his espresso. The plan he'd devised would rid him of both problems. He would handle Isabel Peters far more deftly than she'd tried to handle him. He would take what he wanted and walk away. And he was going to enjoy every minute of it.

A knock sounded on the door. Grace slipped in, set a pile of papers on his desk and turned her curious gaze on him. "Isabel Peters is here."

"Thanks. Show her in."

He leaned against the front of his solid wooden desk as Izzie appeared in the doorway, wearing a simple green dress that hugged her lush figure. He zeroed in on the stiff set of her face and shoulders. She was nervous. Good.

He gestured toward the sitting area by the windows. "Have a seat."

She walked past him and perched on the corner of one of the matching leather chairs. He sauntered over and sat opposite her, deliberately letting silence reign until she squirmed in her seat.

"What made you change your mind?"

"My management team thinks we need the public on our side."

"You'll do the interview then?"

He nodded. "With a few conditions."

A guarded look replaced the relieved glimmer in her eyes. "Which are?"

"We have complete control over the final edit."

"That'll never happen."

"Then you won't get the interview."

She frowned. "What else?"

"You'll be the reporter."

"James assigned the story to me. It's mine."

He sat back and crossed his arms over his chest. "That part I don't understand. The community reporter doing an investigative feature? Working your way up the ladder Hollywood-style, Iz?"

She clenched her hands in her lap, fire flashing in her dark eyes. "What's it going to take for you to believe the truth? I didn't know it was you, Alex."

"Give it up," he encouraged in a bored tone. "We're wasting time here. What I am interested in," he said deliberately, "is if you're still part of the package?"

Her face turned the exact color of his fire-engine-red Ferrari. "That was way over the line."

"Too bad," he gibed. "I'm in the driver's seat now. You *need* me."

She looked down at her hands, twisted them together in her lap. "You said a few conditions…"

He nodded. "I'm assuming you want to get started on the interview right away?"

She inclined her head.

"I have business in California this week," he drawled. "You'll need to come with me."

Her mouth fell open. "I—we—I can't do that. We can do the pre-interviews by phone."

He shook his head. "We do it in person or we don't do it at all."

She chewed on her lip, uncertainty glittering in those big brown eyes. "What's the matter?" he goaded. "You were all over me that night in London."

"That was real," she hissed. "This has to be strictly business now."

He moved his gaze leisurely over her curves in the sexy, understated dress. "Why, when we clearly mix business and pleasure so well?"

Her back went ramrod straight. "That's enough."

A slow smile stretched his lips. "I recognize ambition, Iz. I get it. I'm ruthless too. Why not scratch the itch? Get it out of our systems?"

She flashed him a heated look. "If we do this it's business."

He crossed one leg over the other in an indolent gesture. "Does your boss know we've slept together? How far you decided to take it? Or was that just because you were enjoying it and you made the call?"

She stood up. "I'm done with this conversation."

"Get your bag packed, Iz." He rolled to his feet. "We leave tomorrow morning."

"I can't do that." She gaped at him. "I have stories I'm working on."

"Hand them off," he ordered, striding over to his desk. "Grace will call you with the details. Oh," he added, sitting down in his chair. "Don't forget your bathing suit. The pool is spectacular."

Her mouth tightened. She walked out without a backward glance. He smiled and pulled a file toward him. He'd bet his Ferrari Izzie looked amazing in a bikini. He couldn't wait to find out.

CHAPTER EIGHT

SHE REALLY SHOULD get out of the sun, Izzie thought lazily, staring up at the perfect, clear blue California sky. Except after the stress of the past couple of days, heaven right now was floating on her back in Alex's infinity pool and escaping the heat.

She sighed and trailed her hands through the water. It was one of those sweat-inducing, steaming-hot summer California days that made everyone go a little crazy. So she'd done what any self-respecting native Californian would have done while Alex was in San Francisco in meetings and the ever-present tension between them was gone for a few hours. She'd headed outside to the pool, armed with a pitcher of cold lemonade and a book.

She should get out of the sun. And she would soon. It was just that the infinity pool with its gasp-inducing, hundred-foot drop to the Pacific was like teetering on the edge of heaven. In fact, everything about Alex's excessively private Spanish-style home perched over the wildly beautiful golden beaches of Malibu was heavenly. Acres of tropical gardens swamped the grounds with color, its expansive outdoor living spaces encouraging one to spend all their time outside. And then there was the house, with the works of the great Impressionists on the walls.

She flicked her hand through the water and sent an arc

of diamond-shaped drops through the air. It was a privileged, luxurious slice of paradise, as elusive to most as the man she'd been interviewing all week. Four days into their stay, three days into their background interviews, and she still knew so little about the man behind the trophies she was afraid to pick up James's calls. That night in London hadn't been an outlier. Alex didn't talk about himself. Had given one-line answers to every question she'd asked and nothing more.

She shut her eyes against the blinding rays of the sun, sweat dripping down her forehead and beneath her lashes. Alex was hosting a party for business associates tomorrow, after which she was headed back to New York, with or without the story. Which meant today she had to get him to talk. A near impossible task when your interview subject had zero trust in you.

She waved her arms and pushed herself back to the center of the pool. She'd done everything she could to convince Alex she was telling the truth but it was like talking to a wall. The man she'd met in London was gone. And the aloof stranger who'd replaced him unnerved her. So did the ever-present heat between them. He might hate her for what she'd done, but he still wanted her. That hadn't gone away. It'd made her flee dinner on the intimate little terrace last night like a woman possessed.

Twenty-four hours, she told herself. Twenty-four hours and she'd be out of danger. But she needed him to talk first.

"You researching cloud formations?"

The sardonic observation from a deep, amused male voice had her yanking herself upright and feeling for the bottom. But the water was too deep and she plunged, her arms and legs flailing. Kicking back to the surface, she pulled in a breath, coughing and sputtering.

"Do you always sneak up on people like that?"

"I thought you said you were a champion swimmer..."

"That doesn't help when you scare the life out of me." She pushed her soaking hair out of her face and took in yet another of the gorgeous designer suits that molded every lean muscle of his body into a work of art.

His gaze slid over her. She'd put her minuscule bikini on while he was out. *What had possessed her to do that?*

He shrugged out of his jacket and threw it on a lounger. "Don't you have piles of research to do? Five miles to run? Fifty laps to swim?"

She eyed him. "You're one to talk. You never stay still either."

"Yes, but I do know how to relax." He sank down on his haunches beside the edge of the pool. "This," he said, nodding his head toward her, "gives me hope for the control freak in you."

"I am not a control freak."

"Sure you are." He whipped off his tie and threw it on top of his jacket. "You even eat with everything perfectly segmented. Meat first, potatoes next, vegetables last."

Her cheeks, already warm from the heat of the sun, got about five degrees hotter. "That's because I like the vegetables the least. That doesn't equal a control freak."

"Says a lot about a person." His gaze sharpened on her. "In London, you said you've always been afraid of things blowing up in your face." He tipped his head to one side. "What are you afraid of now, Izzie? That you'll give in to this heat between us?"

Yes, she thought desperately. She pulled her gaze resolutely away from his. "I was just about to get out. Can we start early then? We have a lot of ground to cover."

"Sure." He held out a hand.

She shook her head. "I'll get out in a sec. You go change first."

He gave her a thoughtful look. "You don't want to get out of the pool in that bikini, do you?"

Damn right she didn't.

"Coward," he mocked. "I've seen you naked. What's a bikini?"

She surveyed the distance between her and the stairs at the other end of the pool.

"You'll never make it."

She looked back at him. He was *laughing* at her. "Okay, you've had your fun. Go inside, change and we'll meet back here."

"Nicely asked but no. I can't leave you unattended in the pool. I could be sued if anything happens to you."

"That's ridiculous," she sputtered. "I've been out here for ho—"

He grabbed her arm and hauled her dripping up onto the pool deck. "Problem solved."

Problem started. Heat flared between them, her soaking-wet body dripping all over his designer suit as he kept a firm grip on her wrist. "Alex—"

"All week you've been sending out these mixed signals, Iz." He released her wrist to slide a hand around her waist and pull her closer. "Which is it—you want me or you don't?"

"Don't." She pressed a hand hard against his chest and shoved him away. "You are the most egocentric—" She stopped in her tracks as he rocked back on his heels to steady himself, sidestepped to keep his balance, missed the concrete entirely and fell into the pool.

Her hands flew to her mouth as he came to the surface, biting out some choice swear words. "Oh my God, I'm so sorry, I didn't mean to do that."

He swiped the water from his face, slicking his dark hair back. "Somehow I find that hard to believe."

She shoved her hands on her hips. "It's your fault. I'm trying to keep things business between us…"

"Liar," he muttered, wading toward the steps, his wet

clothes weighing him down. "You've been wondering as much as I have what it would be like to do it again."

"Doesn't mean I'm going to," she growled. She picked up her towel, threw it on the pool deck for him and stalked inside past the flabbergasted-looking housekeeper who was standing with a tray of drinks in her hands watching Alex climb out of the pool.

A much calmer, pulled-together Izzie returned to the terrace ten minutes later, showered and composed. Alex had changed into a similar outfit to hers—shorts and a T-shirt that did a whole lot for his tanned, muscular legs and washboard abs. She resolutely removed her gaze from him. *No more mixed signals.* "Ready?"

He nodded and led the way down the steep set of stairs to the beach. She'd suggested a walk instead of their usual session on the terrace, thinking maybe if she wasn't sitting across from him with a pad of paper and a tape recorder, he'd open up.

At the bottom of the old wooden stairs, she kicked off her shoes and sank her toes into the sand. Alex did the same and they started walking.

"Did you manage to meet your dad for lunch?"

She nodded.

"How is he?"

"He's...fine. Better than I've seen him for a while."

"Did he ever find someone else? After your mother left?"

She shook her head. "I wish he would."

"Why do you think he hasn't?"

"I think he's still in love with my mother."

"After all this time?"

"Crazy, huh?"

His gaze sharpened on her face. "You think he's a fool?"

She threw him a sideways look. "She destroyed him when she walked out. She never deserved him. So yes, I do."

Her sweet, loving father had worshipped the ground her mother had walked on. He'd been doing the music for one of her films when they'd met and fallen head over heels for the beautiful, charismatic actress. Unfortunately, he'd idealized her as the silver screen legend she was rather than the flawed woman he'd married. Had never wanted to see how unhappy she was with small-town life in Palo Alto until the day she'd walked out the door. Her stomach twisted. The sight of their father falling apart wasn't one two teenage girls should have had to deal with. And yet they had.

"The blame is rarely one-sided." Alex kicked a sharp seashell out of the way, the still-scorching hot sun pouring down on them. "Marry two people long enough and they'll find a way to hate each other."

"Wow. I thought I was cynical."

"If you've done your homework you'll know my parents' marriage was disastrous."

She had. Knew Hristo and Adelphe Constantinou had separated when Alex was a teenager and his mother had married another very rich man in a scandal that had rocked New York society.

"It was not a nice divorce," she commented.

"It was not. Are we on the record now?"

"Yes."

She watched the now-familiar shield come down over his face, wiping his expression clean of emotion. As it did every time things turned personal.

"Tell me about your relationship with your father."

"That has nothing to do with this story."

"I disagree." She shot him a sideways look. "You need

to start talking to me, Alex, or we'll go with Messer's story and leave you out."

He lifted his shoulders. "That might be tough when your boss wants my story, not Messer's."

True. But he still needed to talk. She pressed her lips together. "I get that your PR person wants you to stay on message. But you have to give me something. You know we want to highlight your football background and for that I need to understand your beginnings."

A frown creased his brow. "My father was a workaholic who spent every waking hour of his life building C-Star Shipping. He didn't care about anyone or anything that didn't involve his company. End of story."

Ouch. So the rumors about Alex and Hristo Constantinou's relationship were true. "What caused the falling-out between you and your father?"

"We had a philosophical disagreement about whether or not I would run C-Star Shipping," he said flatly. "We parted ways after that."

"What do you mean, parted ways?"

His expression went from blank to ice-cold. "I mean we parted ways."

The rumor was that Hristo had disowned him. She'd thought it was just some crazy angle the press had blown up, but apparently it was true. Wow. She was speechless for a moment, the black-and-white of it all blowing her away. When she'd been a teenager, she would have died for the talent and charisma to follow in her mother's footsteps. The heir apparent to run C-Star Shipping, Alex had chosen to follow his own path and his father had disowned him for it. It was as though you couldn't win no matter what you did. Or maybe that was just when you had megalomaniac parents like theirs? Hristo Constantinou was an autocrat who ruled his empire with an iron fist. Had Alex's insubordination simply been too much for him to take?

"What did your mother think of all this? Didn't she have any say in it?"

"She was out of the picture by then. She'd married Jack Sinclair and my father never gave her any true power in the company despite all the family money she sank into it."

"What about your sisters? Why couldn't they have taken the reins?"

His mouth curled. "My father would never have put a woman at the helm."

"What are they like, your sisters?" She asked the question more out of curiosity than a need to know.

His face took on a decidedly softer edge. "They're all completely different. Agape, whose dress you wore, she's the oldest, an event planner in New York. Bubbly, always talking too much. Gabby is a librarian, has middle-child syndrome. Always trying to please everyone. And Arty—" his mouth curved as Izzie gave him a curious look "—short for Artemis, and yes my mother really called her that, and yes we teased her about it and called her a goddess her entire life, is finishing up her final year at law school. Whip smart."

She smiled. "They sound completely different. Which one are you closest to?"

He shrugged. "All of them, really. They came to live with me when I turned pro. Agape and I are the most alike, I guess."

"Agape is the one coming tomorrow night?"

"Yes. She helped me plan the party."

Which reminded her that her time to get him to talk was running out. She dug in. "Back to Frank Messer then. You've said Mark created *Behemoth*. Messer claims he did. How do you reconcile that?"

"Developing a game like *Behemoth* involves hundreds of people. Come take a tour of our development facility. It's mind-boggling how much work goes into a title. For *years.* Messer played a key role, yes, but so did dozens of other designers. The platform, the *starting point*, was Mark's vision. The patents rightfully belong to Sophoros."

"Then why did you pay him off?"

He scowled. "We were rewarding him for everything he'd put into the company. He deserved it for his tenure."

"He says you took unfair advantage of him. Bullied him into it."

"Funny he should be saying that now when the game is a raging success." Sarcasm dripped from his voice. "He was fine enough with the money before."

"He says he has proof *he* created the platform."

"Then let him bring it forward. It doesn't exist."

Fine. She was starting to get that feeling the more unforthcoming Messer became on that point. She took a deep breath. "I need to ask you about the night your career ended."

A wary expression slid over his face. "What's there to ask? I came back too soon, tore my rotator cuff and it was over."

She bit down on her lip. Forced herself to go on. "I talked to your coach, Brian Sellers. And to Dr. Forsyth. They both said you weren't supposed to play that night, Alex. Dr. Forsyth had given you strict orders to stay on the bench for at least another month. And Sellers had backed him up."

His jaw tightened. "I felt fine so I decided to play."

She struggled to keep up with him as his strides lengthened. "But why would you do that? You'd told Coach Sellers you weren't going to play. Why risk your career?"

He stopped in his tracks, the hint of a storm brewing in his blue eyes. "I thought I was fine. I made a mistake. That's all there is to it."

She pressed sweaty palms to her thighs, telling herself to just get it over with. "But Gerry Thompson was already starting. You didn't have to go out there. Surely your career was more important than one game?"

"What the hell would you know about it?" he roared, his sudden explosion making her take a step back in the sand. His eyes blazed, skin stretched taut across his cheekbones. "How could you have any idea about the pressure I was under? About what I was risking by *not* playing? The media—*you,*" he said, pointing a finger at her, "you wanted my head on a platter."

Izzie's heart was pounding as if it were going to jump out of her chest, but she pressed on. "You needed to prove to your father you could be a success. You played because failure was not an option."

"I didn't care what the hell my father thought," he ground out. "*Christós,* Izzie, have you listened to a word I've said? I thought I was fine so I played. That's it."

"I know about the illegal painkillers." She forced the words past her constricted throat. "I know you had someone supply you with a street-level narcotic that allowed you to play that night…that allowed you to mask your injury. That there were some who worried you might have become…*dependent* on it."

His tanned face turned ashen. "Who told you that?"

"I can't reveal my source."

He stood there utterly silent, feet spread apart, fists clenched at his sides, the absolute devastation on his face shaking her to the core. But it was nothing compared to the look of white-hot rage that was spreading across it now, making her breath catch in her throat, making her take another step backward.

When he finally spoke, it was in a voice so lethally quiet she had to strain to hear it over the crash of the waves.

"We are done with this conversation. I will answer the question about why I played on camera next week, at which time I'll give the answer I just did. And that will be the last

time it's mentioned, *ever*, or this story will not happen."
He trained his gaze on her face. *"Do you understand?"*

She nodded, hands, knees, everything shaking as he
stalked down the beach away from her. Her brain spun.
How could one night have possibly been more important
than an entire golden career? Brian Sellers had charac-
terized Alex as a man who'd never taken an unsure step
in his life. So what had happened that night to push him
over the edge? To make him play when there was no way
he should have ever taken a step onto that field?

CHAPTER NINE

THIRTY LAPS OF his fifty-metre pool was generally pretty cathartic for Alex. But after spending the last twenty-four hours ruminating over yesterday's conversation with Izzie and facing demons he'd thought long ago put to bed, it wasn't having the desired effect.

Biceps crying out from the vicious workout, he stepped out of the shower, toweled himself off and stalked into the bedroom where he rifled through his closet for his tuxedo shirt. He should have listened to his instincts and never agreed to do the interview. Because those questions Izzie had asked yesterday, the pieces of his past she was digging up, were nobody's business but his own. She and James Curry were clearly taking this interview in a whole different direction from what they'd agreed upon, and the private life he'd guarded so closely for so long was in danger of being blown wide open by a woman he had severely conflicting feelings about.

He jammed his hand against the closet door, dropped his head and let out a string of curses. *How had Izzie found out about the illegal painkillers?* The only person who knew he'd taken them was his former teammate, Xavier Jones. And Xavier wouldn't have talked to a reporter. No way.

But then again, he thought, agitation rocketing through him, what did it really matter now? His football career was history. He'd paid for his mistake in the worst way possible. And he'd moved on. He didn't *need* football anymore.

So why did he feel gutted? As if someone had sliced him wide open? *Because the only thing worse than reliving it all over*, a little voice in his head said, *would be to be made into a pity party all over again.* To have the whole world know his shame. He'd worked too hard building Sophoros into an international powerhouse to let the media make a tragedy of him a second time. To overshadow everything he'd done since.

He would not let it happen. *Could not.*

He yanked his shirt out of the closet, found some boxers, and pulled them on. He would do exactly as he'd said. He'd do this interview, he'd draw the lines, then he'd never talk about it again. No one could prove anything. And as for Izzie? He grimaced as he did up the finicky little pearl buttons on the shirt. He was at a loss. Ever since she'd walked into his life, she'd been driving him slowly, surely mad. And it wasn't getting any better. When he should be thinking about Frank Messer and the case his lawyers were mounting against him, he was wondering instead how to get her into bed. How to satisfy the craving in him that ached for another taste of her.

His shirt finally done up, he located his tuxedo trousers, pulled them on and went searching for his bow tie. He should hate Izzie for setting him up. For digging into his painful past. But the satisfaction of harboring that against her was being called into question after the conversation he'd had with Laura Reed this morning. He and his head of PR had been covering some items that couldn't wait until he was back in New York when Laura's tone had changed into that serious, "you need to listen to me" one she reserved for the most important points. "Alex," she'd censured. "I met James Curry at an industry breakfast this morning. He asked me what the deal was with you.

Said you tore into him at the Met fund-raiser about him setting you up...and he still couldn't figure out what you were talking about."

"The guy's an underhanded son of a bitch," he'd replied. "Let's leave it at that."

"He's an important son of a bitch," Laura had reminded him drily. "He's the news director at one of New York's most influential television stations. You want him on your side. I don't know what issue you have with him, but he's a straight shooter, Alex. In my ten years of working with him I've never seen him do anything unethical. Set anyone up. So whatever you're thinking, you're wrong. Kiss and make up and play nice."

He'd muttered something to pacify her, then moved on. But the conversation had been playing over in his head ever since. Izzie had steadfastly stuck to her story that their meeting in the elevator had been a coincidence. His receptionist in London had confirmed she'd lied to Izzie about his whereabouts to get rid of her per his standing instructions to do so. Which left him wondering if maybe their elevator meeting *had* just been a bizarre coincidence.

He located his shoes and jammed his feet into them without care for the supple Italian leather. Izzie was up for a big promotion at NYC-TV. It explained why she'd been so desperate to land this story on Sophoros. And made the heavy weight sitting in his chest sink even deeper. *What if his paranoia about the media had led him to a completely wrong judgment of Izzie?* What if she *was* the woman he'd thought he'd met that night in London? And if she was, what did that mean?

His mind buzzing, he recalled the look of complete incomprehension on Curry's face that night at the Met when he'd accused him of setting him up. Izzie's frantic attempts to hide the fact that they'd slept together. *Curry hadn't known.*

He picked up his watch and strapped it around his wrist. Had that night in London been so intense, so real for him that he'd been willing to believe the worst about Izzie to avoid making the same mistake twice? A search for any reason not to fall for another woman as hard as he had Jess?

He glanced at the clock and gave his head a shake. He had a black-tie party for a hundred people to get through on a night when he'd rather do anything but. But his bigger problem by far was Isabel Peters. And what the hell he was going to do with her.

If there was anything she *should* be good at, it was the fine art of negotiating a cocktail party. Izzie plucked a glass of champagne off a passing waiter's tray and perched herself against a tree in the lantern-lit gardens of Alex's Malibu hideaway. Years of reluctantly attending her mother's premieres and engagements, not to mention the local events the station sponsored, *should* make this all second nature to her. Instead she tended to feel like a fish out of water, always the gauche, awkward daughter of Dayla St. James who did not thrive in the spotlight.

She took a sip of the bubbly, dry vintage, taking in Agape's party planning genius. Alex's sister had done an amazing job transforming the pool and garden area into a lush, exotic oasis—as if you'd entered the Garden of Eden on a particularly electric, sensual night. Flaming torches glowed around the outskirts of the gardens, and floral-shaped candles floated on the pool, casting a muted glow across its surface. And the breezy, lazy music coming from the hip-looking DJ in the corner was typical laid-back California cool.

She frowned. She might actually have enjoyed a party for a change if she weren't wound so tight she felt as though she was going to snap in half. Her confrontation with Alex yesterday had left her shaken—utterly unsure what to do.

She had the true story about what had happened on the last night of his career. At least *most* of it. Had an explosive angle that would ensure a headline story. But she wasn't sure she could do it. Wasn't sure she could blow Alex's life apart like that.

Letting out a long breath, she leaned back against the pillar and scanned the crowd for him. Long, lean and outrageously handsome in a perfectly tailored tux, he was chatting with a group of people in the center of the buzzing, affluent crowd that, according to Agape, consisted of everything from film directors to financiers to every type of entertainment industry professional in between.

She studied the tension written across his strongly carved features. Brooding, tunnel-visioned since their confrontation yesterday, he'd avoided her completely. And she wondered why she just couldn't stay immune to him. Why her pulse, even now, raced in a zigzag of confusion.

What was it about a brooding, fabulously good-looking man that made you want him to turn all that intensity on you? Even if you knew it was a *bad, bad* idea?

He turned his head, their gazes meeting and holding. Her breath caught in her throat as an emotion other than anger flickered in his eyes. Desire? Confusion? She'd been expecting hatred. Antagonism. Not this.

Her mouth went dry as he worked his way down over the sexy spaghetti-strap dress she'd bought in Malibu today to fit the occasion. To catch his attention if she was honest. And why do that? Why play with fire *now,* when she was so close to escape?

She swallowed hard. It was *irresistible*.

He moved the heated intensity of his gaze back up to her face. Electricity arced between them, along with thoughts of a career-ending variety. How much damage would one more night do if no one ever knew? And how could she even be *thinking* that, now of all times?

And then it came to her. What she should have known from the beginning…she had never been nor would she ever be objective when it came to Alex Constantinou. She could not turn his personal tragedy into the most-watched interview of the year. Whatever had made him play that night, take those drugs, it didn't belong in her story. It didn't belong in anyone's story.

Someone grabbed a hold of Alex's arm and commanded his attention. She exhaled a long, shaky breath. And suddenly knew exactly what she was going to do. She was going to bury the information. Tell James he was going to have to go with a different angle. And in doing so throw away her best chance at landing this anchor job. At making her career.

Her trembling fingers bit into her glass to keep it from falling to the ground. A cold knot formed in her stomach. She was risking her job. Her vow to tell the truth no matter what. For a man who thought she was a cold-hearted opportunist. *Nice one, Izzie.*

She made it through the next couple of hours in a muted haze as the party wound down and the crowd began thinning out. Agape was witty and charming and they hit it off. Debated the merits of some of the eligible men in the crowd. She was at her side when the last few guests made their way toward the driveway and Agape declared herself done.

"Walk me out?" she said to Izzie. "We'll have to do drinks when we're back in New York."

She said goodbye to Agape. Found herself standing beside Alex as he waved her off and finished chatting with the last remaining guest, the CEO of an offshore drilling company that operated off the coast of California. The sideways look he gave her as the taillights of Agape's bright red convertible zigzagged down the driveway had her stepping backward.

The weight of his hand came down on her shoulder. "Don't even think about it," he muttered under his breath. She stood there while he shook the CEO's hand, her heart-beat accelerating in a painful mixture of fear and anticipation. The tall Southerner clapped Alex on the back, folded himself into his sports car and drove off.

She cleared her throat. "Alex, I'm really tired. Maybe we can—"

He squared to face her. "If you don't think we're settling this tonight, you *are seriously* deluded, Izzie."

Her breath caught in her throat. The heat of his palm burned into the bare skin of her shoulder as he marched her toward the house.

"Stay put," he instructed, when they reached the legions of catering staff packing up in the pool area. He disappeared, then came back with a bottle of champagne and two glasses. Her heart beat like a snare drum as he propelled her toward the back of the house.

"Where are we going?"

He gave her a sideways look. "I thought you'd prefer doing this in private rather than broadcasting it to every gossip magazine in L.A."

Good point. She picked up her pace to keep up as he turned the corner of the house and headed for the terrace off his master suite. The sheer drop to the Pacific was gob-smackingly gorgeous. Her stomach felt as though it was going down along with it.

Alex deposited the bottle and glasses on the table and stripped off his jacket. The lump in her stomach increased to the size of a grapefruit. He shot her a sideways look. "Why don't you open the champagne?"

His quietly spoken words struck her as glaringly symbolic. She went completely still, studying the expression on his face. Searching for the softening she'd seen earlier.

"I know you didn't set me up, Izzie."

Her eyes widened. "How?"

"I talked to Laura Reed this morning and she gave me an earful. Said James was the type who plays by the rules. That setting me up wasn't something he would do."

"But you didn't believe that before," she said slowly. "Why now?"

He shrugged and loosened his tie. "I'm a little—a lot," he corrected, "paranoid about the media. They've made my life hell with their lies and speculation. And sometimes I get a little crazy about it." He pulled off the tie and slung it over a chair. "After I talked to Laura, I remembered how desperately you tried to get James to leave that night at the Met, and I realized he had no idea about us. Then my rational brain finally kicked in. It isn't you, Izzie."

She caught her lip between her teeth. "You really believe me?"

"Yes."

Bewildered, she let it sink in. Felt a warm feeling spread through her, relief mixed with something else. It had *killed* her to think he believed her capable of that after what they'd shared. She swallowed hard and lifted her gaze to his. "I'm giving up the story."

His brows pulled together. "Why?"

"I'm not objective about you, Alex, I never have been."

His mouth twisted. "You've been doing a pretty good job of giving Frank Messer a fair shake."

She shook her head. "It's not that. I— I'm burying the information about the illegal drugs. You don't need to worry about it."

He stared at her. "Why?"

Because I fell for you so hard that night in London I can't see straight. She lifted her chin and said instead, "Because I can't do that to you."

"You're up for a promotion. You need this story."

She shrugged. "Some things in life are more important than a story."

"Your boss would disagree."

Her stomach twisted. "He would disagree with just about everything I've done thus far. I think I have a bit of soul-searching to do."

He undid his cuff and rolled it back. "An anchor job is going to be a hell of a lot of pressure, Izzie. Cutthroat competition."

"You did it, being a quarterback."

"I thrive on pressure. It's in my DNA. I don't think you're built like that."

No, she wasn't. What she loved was working in the community every day, telling people's stories. But an anchor job was a once-in-a-lifetime opportunity. And a lot could be done to better the community from that position as well. Maybe more.

She absorbed the roar of the Pacific beneath them. Suddenly everything seemed very, very out of control.

She reached for the champagne, pulled the foil off and worked the cork out with shaking fingers. Amber liquid sloshed over the side of the glass as she poured.

"Izzie." Alex moved behind her and pried the bottle from her fingers. "What's going on?"

Inhaling deeply, she breathed in the sexy, spicy smell of him, the undertone of musky male that was all Alex. And knew she hadn't truly thought of anything but being back in his arms for weeks.

He turned her around. Watched her with that all-seeing gaze of his until she shook her head and gave him an uncertain smile. "Do you know what's funny? I promised myself I would never, *ever* let a man get in the way of my career. And now not only am I doing that," she said, her voice holding more than a trace of irony, "but I'm doing it at the most important moment of my career."

He reached up and ran his thumb across her cheek. "Don't you know control is a myth? None of us are in control of anything, Iz. Not over that elevator we were in and not over this thing between you and me."

His words hit her with soul-destroying precision. Knocked down every last barrier she had. Because he was right. And believing any less made a mockery of the promise she'd made to herself that night in London.

She tipped her head back to look up at him, the fog in her brain clearing. "We still have the issue that I'm a reporter and you hate them."

"I'm willing to suspend judgment on that." He dragged his thumb down over the soft skin of her throat to the throbbing pulse at the base of her neck. "Because this particular reporter," he said softly, "I like very much."

"Alex—" She pressed a hand against his chest. "That night in London the rules were clear-cut. We said it was one night and I— I could handle that. But this—" she shook her head "—I'm pretty sure I'm out of my league right about now..."

He reached up and laced his fingers through the hand she had pressed against his chest. "I'm pretty sure I am too."

She stared at him. "What do you mean?"

He released her hand and drew her to him. She pulled in a shaky breath as he cupped her face in his palm. "I told myself I shouldn't touch you that night in London because I knew with you it was going to be different. That I wasn't going to be able to walk away afterward like I always do."

"But you did."

He nodded. "That morning when I left, I was *running*, Iz. I thought if I ran fast enough I could ignore what I was feeling. But it didn't work. I almost picked up the phone a dozen times before I saw you that night at the Met."

She tried to keep her wits about her as he slid a hand

into her hair and tipped her head back. "How about we start over?" he suggested softly, this stripped-down, open version of Alex doing crazy things to her common sense. "A blank slate. No expiration dates. No rules. And see where it goes."

It was…crazily, frantically tempting. "But you don't do 'let's see where this goes.'"

"I don't have a choice with you," he admitted huskily, lowering his head until his mouth brushed against hers. "I think that's pretty clear."

For the second time in little more than two weeks Izzie Peters went with her gut and made a massive decision with major repercussions. But this time she was hoping it was going to last more than one night.

She lifted up on tiptoes, swayed into him and let him take her mouth in a hot, sensuous kiss that pulled her into a deep, dark vortex she never wanted to emerge from. She reached up and cupped his jaw with her fingertips, her lips clinging to his as he changed angles, tasted her as if he couldn't get enough.

And when that wasn't enough, she indulged her need to touch the rock-hard body that had been far too temptingly on display this past week. Sank her fingertips into the hard, thick muscles of his shoulders. Slid them down over his pecs, those washboard abs.

Alex groaned. Dragged her closer. "Izzie," he said thickly, "let me take you to bed."

She tipped her head back to look up at him. "Yes," she agreed, the smoky, seductive tone of her voice sounding completely foreign to her.

Fire burned in his eyes. He picked her up and carried her inside, striding through the sitting room and into the bedroom. "One second," he murmured, setting her down on the huge king-size bed. He disappeared, then came back with the champagne bottle.

"I *really* don't need any of that," she said, pressing damp palms against her thighs as she knelt on the bed in front of him.

"Who said we were going to drink it?"

Heat raced to her cheeks. Her body trembled like a violin. She was *so* not prepared for this. She gulped in a breath as he set the bottle on the floor beside the bed and sank his knee down between her thighs. Then moved her fingers to the buttons of his shirt. "Take it off," he invited, his voice dropping to that of a sensually charged invitation. "And I'll show you."

She followed his command, doing only a marginally better job than she had that night in London, but finally it was off, exposing his magnificent abs. Her heart skittered in her chest as he leaned down and took her mouth in a slow, hard kiss, a vision of him as a conquering lord flashing through her head as he arched her neck back and showed no mercy. Except this wasn't one of her paperback novels...this was full-on reality.

His teeth nipped at her bottom lip, demanding entry at the same time he slid his palms down over the small of her back, over her hips and thighs, then brought them back up, sliding underneath her dress to close over the rounded curve of her bare bottom.

"Theos." He lifted his gaze to hers, color staining his cheekbones. "I spent the whole night wondering if you were wearing anything under this."

"I couldn't."

His hands tightened on her hips, lifted her so she was straddling him. She shivered as he settled her against his hard erection, her brain shutting down completely. The need to move against him, to press her sensitized flesh against the hard ridge of him, was undeniable. He felt amazing.

"Izzie," he said hoarsely, "you need to stop that or this is going to happen way too fast."

But she was drunk on how he was making her feel, how she was making *him* feel, and she didn't want to slow down. She wanted fast, wanted to ride the tidal wave of lust sweeping her forward. Sliding back, she moved her hands to his belt and yanked it open. His swift intake of breath as she undid the button of his pants and slid the zipper down emboldened her. His curse as her fingers brushed against the hard length of him made her smile.

She reached into his boxers and freed him. *"Izzie,"* he groaned. "You need to be ready for me. I'm too big for you to—"

She put her fingers to his mouth. "Shut up."

His eyes darkened to that deep cobalt-blue she could drown herself in. He sat back, braced his arms on the bed and watched as she lifted her dress and brought the aroused, hard length of him against her hot, aching flesh. *God.* She closed her eyes. He was so big. How exactly was she going to accomplish this?

Alex caught her hand in his, brought it to his mouth and pressed a kiss against her palm. Her eyes fluttered open, telegraphed her fear. His lips curved in a tortured smile. "Slowly, sweetheart. Take me slowly and it'll be fine."

The fact that Izzie had never been in love before didn't stop her from thinking she might be falling madly in love with Alex rather than just *seeing where this went,* such was the soul-destroying tenderness of that gesture. Taking a deep breath, refusing to go *there*, she reached down and guided him inside her, taking him inch by inch as she'd done before. But in this position, he felt bigger, thicker. And the sensation as she sank down on him was incredible.

She let out a sigh of pleasure. He gave her a strained look. "Good?"

She nodded, finding it almost unbearably intimate to be joined with him like this while he watched her with a heavy-lidded desire that made her insides quiver. Squeezing her eyes shut, she started to move, rotate her hips, taking him deep inside her, then shallower, establishing a rhythm that made him groan. He caught her chin in his fingers. "Look at me, Iz. I want to see your face."

She did. Because something in him grounded her. Always had. She let the heat, the focus in his gaze as she rode him, excite her unbearably. Make her experiment. The thick muscles of his biceps flexed against the bed. "*Theos,*" he bit out in a raw voice. "You feel so good…I'm not sure how long I can stand this."

"Let go," she whispered. Rode him harder, faster, until his breath was coming in short, shallow spurts and his dark lashes swept down over his eyes. She wanted to make him come apart for her. To feel that control. She pressed down on him hard, taking him even deeper inside of her, the friction as she took him again and again so delicious she was getting close…so close…

"Izzie," he groaned, his hips driving up into her now, setting the pace. "I need to— I can't—"

She sank her fingers into the hard muscles of his shoulders, felt his body swell inside her, shake against her, come apart, his face dropping into the curve of her neck. She held him to her, reveling in how uncontrolled, how complete his release was.

His ragged breathing slowed. He pushed back so he could see her face. "That wasn't how it was supposed to be," he growled, a dark frown slanting its way across his face. "I don't lose control like that."

She bit her lip, dropped her gaze to the dark hair dusting his chest. "I wanted it to be good for you."

He tipped her chin up with his fingers. "You were incredible," he assured her, a gravelly edge to his voice. "You were close?"

She nodded.

He slid his fingers under the straps of her dress and

pushed it off her shoulders with a deliberate movement. "Then let's get things back on course."

Her heart galloped like a high-strung racehorse anticipating extreme excitement. He moved his hands to her thighs and urged her up onto her knees. "Put your hands over your head," he ordered. She obeyed and he yanked her dress off, leaving her clad only in her lacy bra.

He set his palm to her chest and pushed, sending her back into the duvet with a soft *swoosh*. Then he picked up the bottle.

A protest rose in her throat. He wasn't actually going to—

"You're going to ruin your duvet," she breathed as he straddled her, bottle in hand.

"To hell with the duvet," he murmured, tipping the bottle upside down and spilling the amber liquid over her heated flesh. "I always thought Cristal couldn't get any better, but this might change my mind."

"Alex," she protested, raising herself up on her elbows. "I don't think—"

He pushed her back down with a flick of his wrist. "Relax."

Oh. Her stomach churned with anticipation as he put his lips to the curve of her breast where the champagne trail began. Took a lace-covered, champagne-soaked nipple into his mouth and sucked deeply. Her insides twisted, heat flaring in the moist, aroused part of her that had been left unfinished. He lavished the same pleasure on her other breast, driving her higher, making her squirm against the whisper-soft down beneath her.

She bolted upward as he pressed his mouth against the trembling skin of her stomach. "I've never—"

His mouth stilled on her inflamed skin. "Don't tell me that selfish boyfriend of yours didn't indulge you in this either."

She shook her head. He pressed a kiss against the tense muscles of her abdomen. "You are so beautiful, Iz. I want to see, taste every part of you…"

She melted. Completely. Released her anxious grip on her muscles, let him part her thighs and arrange her to his satisfaction…follow the trail of liquid downward to her most sensitive flesh. "Oh," she gasped as he parted her, tasted her, the act so soul-baringly intimate she dug her fingers into the bedding and squeezed her eyes shut. But then the hypersensitivity turned to white-hot pleasure as his tongue began a slow, hot torture that made her hips buck off the bed.

"Easy." He held her down with firm hands as he pleasured her with long, slow strokes of his tongue.

"I can't…I don't—*oh*—" Digging her nails harder into the sheets, she willed herself to accept the pleasure he was offering her. But she was too far gone and when his tongue moved against the hard nub that was the center of her pleasure, she couldn't take any more.

"Alex, please—"

"Shh." He slid a hand under her bottom and lifted her to him. "I know."

And then he was sliding a long finger inside her, stroking deep, adding a whole new layer to her pleasure, and she was jerking in to his hands, begging him to give her release. He did, the magic slide of his fingers tipping her over the edge into an orgasm so intense her entire body shook, her head flinging back against the pillows.

Shivers snaking through her, feeling as though she'd been hit by a ten-ton truck, she lay there trying to catch her breath. Alex slid up her body, rested his elbows on either side of her and ran a finger down her cheek.

"You are full of surprises, Isabel Peters," he drawled softly.

Her cheeks heated fifty shades of red. "You don't do so badly yourself."

He dug his hands under her and scooped her up into his arms and carried her to the en suite bathroom. "We need to shower this off you or you'll be a sticky mess."

We?

He flicked on the taps, ran the water hot and pulled her into the huge walk-in shower with him. She closed her eyes as he washed her with an erotic thoroughness that made her want him all over again. Then he carried her back to his bed and made her wish come true.

Izzie let her head drift to his shoulder, absorbing the feeling of rightness she always felt with this man. How utterly complete and protected he made her feel.

Tomorrow she might wonder if she'd made a huge mistake. Tonight, she didn't care.

CHAPTER TEN

THREE THOUGHTS OCCURRED to Izzie as she woke up in Alex's bed, the vibrant blue of the Pacific sparkling beyond the French doors. She was sprawled on top of him as if she *owned* him. She'd made a huge decision with wide-ranging career implications last night, and she had a flight to catch in a few hours.

The last thought, in particular, had her gingerly detaching herself from him and rolling onto her side to look at the clock on the bedside table. Ten o'clock. She needed to leave in a couple of hours. Plenty of time.

Plenty of time to ruminate over what she'd done.

A glance at the man who was normally out of bed by six confirmed he was still asleep. He looked so sexy with a dusting of early-morning stubble covering his jaw, his long, dark lashes swept down over his cheeks; her heart tripped over itself. *Oh my.*

She collapsed back against the pillows and let out the quietest of sighs. In the space of twenty-four hours, she'd slept with her interview subject, agreed to give up the story of a lifetime and committed to starting over with a man who could and surely would break her heart.

Awesome. Way to go, Izzie. You definitely have your priorities in order.

The cold light of day literally and figuratively crowding in on her, she covered her face with her hands. James was going to flip his lid. But what choice had she had? Ethically, she couldn't have continued to work on a story on a man she was now sure she was head-over-heels infatuated with.

She grimaced. Fingered the fine silk sheet draped over her. James wouldn't see it that way. He'd see it as a foolish, shortsighted decision. A wasted opportunity few ever got. Which brought up the question, what *was* she doing? How had she gone from being an ultra-independent woman who knew the value of providing for herself to a blithering idiot when it came to this man?

Was she in love with Alex?

"That's a pensive look if I've ever seen one."

She jumped at the mockingly spoken words, her gaze flicking to a now fully alert Alex. His slow smile melted her insides. "I'm thinking about my boss's reaction on Monday morning."

"He'll get over it."

She twisted the sheet around her finger. "Everything depends on my anchor appearance now."

He captured her hand in his. "You'll be great."

She stared at her tiny hand wrapped in his much larger one. "I have a history of blowing these things when they matter most."

He lifted a brow.

"My mother set up a big interview for me with a national news show when I was fresh out of school. I blew it badly. It's been my Achilles' heel ever since."

He shook his head. "You're beating yourself up over something that happened when you were still wet behind the ears?"

"It's hard not to when nothing you've ever done lives up to your mother's expectations."

He frowned. "Why do you care so much about what

she thinks? You could spend your whole life looking for parental approval and never get it."

He should know. She retrieved her hand from his. "I'm doing this for myself. *I* need to prove I can do this."

He looked at her for a long moment, then nodded and held out his hand. "Come here."

The dark glitter in his eyes made her pulse quicken. "I have a flight to catch."

"Stay. Fly back on Monday with me."

She shook her head. "I need to get back to New York and talk to James."

"One day isn't going to make a difference. Call him. Tell him I'm being difficult."

"You *are* difficult."

"Then it's the perfect excuse, isn't it?" He rolled her beneath him, his muscular thighs pinning her to the mattress. And then she didn't care about James, her flight or anything but the hedonistic side of her that seemed to have taken over.

Hedonism seemed less than a solid choice on Tuesday morning as Izzie stood in front of her boss in his office, her romantic, off-the-charts-hot weekend with Alex a distant memory in the frantic buzz of the newsroom.

"Tell me you have an update for me," he prompted impatiently, from behind his paper-cup-strewn desk.

Her stomach rolled as though she was on the high seas. "I need you to give the Constantinou story to someone else."

He screwed up his face. "Sorry?"

She picked a spot on the wall several centimeters to the right of his face and kept her eyes glued there. "I need you to give the story to someone else."

He sat up straight. "Why?"

She swallowed hard. "Because Alex and I are involved."

"Define involved."

"Involved."

"You're sleeping with him?"

She nodded.

He raked his hands through his hair and threw her a disbelieving look. "Since when? Was this going on that night at the Met?"

"No." Which was the truth. Technically. She gave him an imploring look. "We confronted our feelings this weekend and I—"

"Dammit, Iz." He slammed his hand on his desk so hard brownish liquid from an old coffee sloshed over a pile of papers. He cursed and shoved them out of the way. "You were *screwing* him while you were supposed to be getting the story?"

She felt the blood drain from her face. "That is *not* what happened. I didn't intend on having anything to do with him and then things—things just happened."

"While you're working on the most important story of your career?" he roared. "How could you be so stupid? You of all people, Iz. You've always put your career first—been clear on your priorities."

Apparently not anymore. She pushed her hair out of her face with a shaky hand. "We have something, James."

Her boss snorted. "He's a man. A goddamned shark. You think you're going to be any different than any of the other woman in this town he's gone through?"

Her chest tightened. "It's done. I can't take it back."

He pressed his hands to his temples and pushed out of his chair, pacing to the other side of the room. "You've been off ever since you came back from Italy. Did you actually get concussed in that elevator? What is wrong with you?"

She wasn't actually sure.

"My God, Izzie." He looked at her disbelievingly. "This story would have given you exactly what you needed to win this anchor job."

She bit her lip. "I'll have to prove myself in the audition."

"That would be the understatement of the year." He let out a long breath. "Did you at least get anything good out of him?"

"Not much," she lied, her insides twisting. "The man is a closed book."

His mouth tightened. "I could make a crude remark right about now but I'm going to abstain."

She wrapped her arms around herself. "Would you rather I'd kept my mouth shut?"

"I'd prefer it if I had my smart, rational reporter back."

Bile climbed the back of her throat. "James—"

He waved her out of his office with a dismissive hand. "I need to figure this out. Go out there and do your job. *If you can.*"

Humiliation and confusion mixed to form a potent cocktail as she left, tail between her legs. She went out, shot her story on a heroic mutt who'd saved an elderly lady from having her purse snatched, filed it on autopilot and escaped home before James could give her one more pained look, as though she was his deviant teenager.

Alex had flown her home this morning, then left immediately on business to Toronto, which left her alone in her cozy little apartment with only her mad actions to keep her company. She poured herself a glass of the emergency chardonnay she kept in the fridge for girlfriend visits, stepped over her still-unpacked suitcase and collapsed on the sofa. She'd done the right thing. She knew she had. She was just going to have to put her head down, knock this audition out of the park, and everything would work out.

Wouldn't it?

Alex Constantinou is a shark. She flinched at James's depiction of the man she'd just thrown a piece of her career away for. Was she was a total idiot? Had her near miss in that elevator spurred deviant behavior rather than the courageous sort she was aiming for? Because right now the shark was out wining and dining a client who could be a six-foot amazon for all she knew. And could she really compete with that?

She groaned and covered her face with a pillow. Those two days in Malibu had made her feel things she'd never even knew existed—mad, unexplainable feelings for a man who was as interesting and smart as he was sexy and gorgeous. When they hadn't been in bed together, they'd spent the day on the beach, gone out to dinner and barbecued on the housekeeper's night off. Their discussions, ranging from politics to classic literature to the science of a good run had proved that their natural chemistry together was just as strong out of bed as in it. But even if they had that, was it enough that she should think she *was* any different? Or was James right and she was risking everything she'd ever wanted for a man who would move on when the wind turned?

An image of her mother walking out the front door of their little bungalow flashed through her head. She'd stood there crying, certain she was leaving for good this time, her father's blank face as he'd tried to fight back tears forever imprinted on her mind.

Her throat ached; her eyes burned at the memory. After that had come the seemingly endless amount of tears her father hadn't been able to hide. His complete and utter dissolution. Her and Ella's attempts to make everything right when nothing was.

She reached for her wine and took a big gulp. *A blank slate. No expiration dates. No rules.* Alex hadn't promised her anything. So where was she getting her carte blanche to throw her master plan away? Her "take care of yourself at all costs" plan that had been suiting her just fine. Depend on nothing. Then no one could hurt you.

She clenched her jaw. Told herself she needed to re-focus and refocus fast on what was going to sustain her. *Her career.* Alex might be in her life, but that didn't mean abandoning all common sense. And now was the perfect time to reset the speedometer—when Mr. Testosterone was out of town.

CHAPTER ELEVEN

IZZIE SAT IN the chair in the makeup room of the studios a week later, her stomach rolling like a ride on the deadliest of roller coasters. Where the week had gone leading up to her anchor appearance, she didn't know. She just knew she didn't feel ready. Didn't know if she'd ever feel ready.

Her gaze flicked to the clock on the wall. Thirty minutes. Actually, to be accurate, twenty-nine minutes, thirty-two seconds, before the fate of her career was decided. Her hand shook as she took a sip of water. No pressure there...

"I'm going light on this, Iz," Macy, NYC-TV's makeup artist, said, sweeping powder over Izzie's nose and forehead. "That mother of yours gave you some perfect skin."

Izzie wished her mother had passed along some of her arrogant self-confidence, too. She could have used some of that right about now. Sixty minutes, she told herself. It was like one measly yoga class. Surely she could do that?

Macy twirled a fluffy brush into some rose-colored powder and ran it along Izzie's cheekbone. She drew back, added some more color to the brush, and eyed her subject. "You look different. Alive...you got a new man or something?"

"Of course it's a man," James grumbled, striding into the makeup room, a bouquet of flowers in his hands. "What else would fry her brain into giving up the story of the year?"

Izzie made a face at him. "Are those from you?"

"Nope. Was on my way over here and said I'd bring them."

She looked up at him. After his initial fury, he'd moved on and put all his energy into prepping her for tonight. She was lucky to have him.

"Thank you for all your support the past few weeks."

The cynicism faded from his face. He deposited the flowers on the counter and rested his elbow on it. "You're going to rock this tonight," he said quietly. "Believe in yourself and do what I know you can do."

A lump grew in her throat. He squeezed her arm and took off to shout something at one of the producers. She looked at the huge bouquet of calla lilies to distract herself. Alex was out of town. Had he remembered what tonight was and sent them? She pulled out the card, her skin going all tingly as she recognized his distinctive scrawl.

"Man's got taste," Macy mused.

"Man's got everything," Izzie muttered. "It's a problem."

"Only if you make it one," Macy drawled.

Izzie slid the card out of the envelope. *Game day is all about adrenaline and how you use it. Channel it. Focus it. And...break a leg. —A.*

She sank her teeth into her bottom lip and stared at the flowers. Now he was showing his sensitive side. *Dammit.*

David Lake, the weekend producer, poked his head into the room. "You just about ready to go?"

Macy swept a neutral color over Izzie's lips. "She's good."

Izzie stood up, her legs feeling like spaghetti, her stomach rolling even worse now.

It's all about adrenaline and how you use it. Channel it. Focus it.

She nodded and swallowed hard. Sixty minutes. She could do this.

* * *

James Curry walked Alex to a back corner of the set. "Izzie's on edge," he murmured. "Whatever you do, don't let her see you."

Alex nodded. "Got it."

Curry gave him a wary look. "Listen, Constantinou—"

"I talked to Laura," Alex cut him off. "I owe you an apology. I was barking up the wrong tree."

"You sure as hell were." James dug his hands in his pockets and fixed his gaze on the monitor. "Glad we got that straight."

The producer counted down to air. Izzie's face was pinched and pale, her hands clasped nervously in front of her as she looked into the camera.

"Come on, Iz," James said quietly. "Let's nail this."

Izzie's cohost, Andrew Michaels, greeted the viewers and introduced Izzie. She smiled and returned the greeting, but her demeanor was stilted, completely unlike her. His stomach tightened. *Come on, Izzie. Relax. Breathe… channel it.*

She started reading the headlines, her voice high and rushed, her gaze fixed on the teleprompter. They rolled a clip. He watched her give herself a mental shake. *That's it. Shrug it off.* She started on another story. This time she spoke slower, more evenly. She still looked tense, but a steadiness had come over her. Curry gave an audible sigh. By the time they went to break she was bantering with Michaels, her usual animated expression on display.

Alex's lips curved. She was going to be okay. Good girl.

He leaned back against the wall and crossed his arms over his chest, wondering what the hell he was doing here anyway. A few hours ago, he'd been in an excruciatingly boring meeting in Boston, trying to focus on the stack of numbers the gray-haired CFO of a consumer electronics retailer was throwing at him, and failing miserably. All he could think about was Izzie and being here for her.

After all, he'd rationalized, who knew better than him what it was like to have your career hang in the balance? To have everything you'd worked for come down to four quarters that flew by in the blink of an eye? So he'd called his old friend he'd had dinner plans with, canceled and hightailed it home.

What he didn't know was what he was actually doing. When two weeks of satisfying your lust with a woman didn't inspire the "it's been fun" speech, a smart man walked.

He wasn't walking.

"And that's a wrap. Thanks, everyone…"

Izzie sat at the anchor desk in a daze as David bounded up onto the set and unclipped her mic. "Great job," he beamed. "It was a really good show."

"Except for the rocky start."

"Nothing you wouldn't have extracted yourself from given a little more experience." Andrew, her cohost, clapped her on the back. "Nice job, Izzie."

Relief swept over her like a tidal wave, her hands and feet tingling under the bright lights. The sweet buzz of victory raced through her veins. It had either been channeling her fear or allowing it to consume her for the rest of her life.

She had done it.

She stood up, walked into James's bear hug. He drew back, a grin on his face. "Lester Davies called me five minutes ago raving about you."

The head of the network?

James grinned. "He apparently missed the first five minutes…"

Her stomach knotted. "It was bad, wasn't it?"

"You loosened up." He jerked his head over his shoulder. "I'd say let's go celebrate but I'm figuring you're gonna choose him over us."

Him? She squinted into the darkness. A tall figure straightened away from the wall. *Alex.*

"We can do our drinks another night," James said gruffly. "Get out of here."

Izzie didn't hesitate, her legs wobbling as she walked toward Alex, but this time for a totally different reason. She stopped in front of him, tipped her head back and looked up at him. "You're supposed to be in Boston."

"I managed to get home early." His mouth tipped up at the sides. "You were great, Iz."

"I got better as I went."

His gaze swept over her. "You look sexy in a suit."

Heat spread through her. "The words on the card were perfect. Thank you."

He nodded toward the crew. "I know I'm barging in on your night, but I have some champagne in the fridge I thought we could...drink."

Her pulse raced. "I'm getting my jacket."

Her feet couldn't seem to move fast enough as she sped back to her desk, switched off her computer and gathered her things. She was turning to leave when she noticed the folded tabloid on her desk. Frowning, she picked it up and flipped it open. And suddenly felt winded. A photo of Alex and a stunningly beautiful brunette coming out of a restaurant together was emblazoned on the front page.

She glanced at the date. Thursday. When he'd said he couldn't see her.

She dragged the paper closer to read the caption.

Former football star and sexy CEO Alex Constantinou had dinner with his former fiancée at Miro's on Thursday night. He and the soon-to-be ex-wife of

Flames quarterback Gerry Thompson looked ultra-cozy together, making us wonder if things are back on.

The warm glow inside her chilled. She stood there, her heart shriveling up into a tiny ball. The sound of hushed voices penetrated her haze. She looked over at the two reporters at the entertainment desk, watching her. *They'd left it for her.*

She turned her back on them. And searched for an explanation. Alex wasn't the type of guy to cheat. He was brutally honest in everything he did.

So why was he having dinner with his ex?

She took a deep breath, shoved the paper in her bag and walked toward the exit. She'd ask him. As a rational woman who wasn't crazy with jealousy would. That was her, right?

"All right, out with it. What's wrong?" Alex threw his keys on the hall table at his penthouse and shut the door.

"I think I've hit the wall," Izzie murmured, no closer to knowing how to bring up the photo than she'd been a half hour ago.

He lifted a brow. "*Now*, Iz."

She walked over to where her bag lay on the floor. "Someone left this on my desk," she said quietly, pulling the tabloid out and handing it to him.

He scanned the story, his mouth tightening as he read. Then he tossed it down on the hall table. "She's going through a tough time with her divorce," he said flatly. "That's *you* people blowing a simple dinner up into something it isn't."

She bit her lip. "Why didn't you tell me it was her that night?"

"Because I thought you'd have the same insecure reaction you're having right now," he bit out. "It was nothing."

She swallowed hard, pressed her damp palms against her thighs. If it was nothing why hadn't he told her? Wasn't she allowed a *little* insecurity over a dinner he'd deliberately kept secret from her? With his *ex?*

"She's obviously still in love with you," she said quietly. "One look at that photo and it's as plain as day."

"There's nothing between Jess and me, Iz. You have to trust me or this is never going to work."

She clenched her hands at her sides, frustration bubbling over. "You can't blame me for asking. Alex, you almost married the woman, then you go out for dinner with her and I find out about it in the tabloids."

He let out a harsh breath. "You of all people should know what they print in those rags is complete crap."

"I do—I just—" She floundered helplessly. "I just wish you'd told me."

He jammed his hands in his pockets. "This is my life, Iz. This is what *you* people have been doing to me my entire life, spinning lies and painting them as truth."

"I am not *you people*. I'm the woman who gave up the story of a lifetime to protect you."

Color stained his high cheekbones. "This is never going to end. It's who I am. What you signed up for by agreeing to be with me. The press love to dish the dirt on my relationships. There'll undoubtedly be more telling their story when the money's right. So if you can't handle it maybe you should get out now."

His words rang out, stark and unrelenting in the quiet stillness of the penthouse. The silence between them stretched to deafening. He spun on his heel and stalked toward the kitchen.

Alex pulled two champagne flutes out of the cupboard, set them on the counter and leaned his forehead against the cool wood. What was he doing? Izzie hadn't deserved that.

But that tabloid had set him off. On the heels of everything else he was dealing with, after that unexpected phone call from Jess this week, it was just too much.

Jess's voice had been raw, thick with tears when she'd caught him on his way out of a meeting. Her marriage to Gerry was falling apart. She needed him. And fool that he was, he'd canceled on Izzie and agreed to meet her for dinner, because no matter what she'd done to him, he'd loved her once and she needed him.

Pressure built in his head, the kind before a thunderstorm that held you in its vise. Once he would have died to hear Jess tell him she still loved him. That she'd made a mistake. Instead it had seemed like some cruel joke that was ten years too late. Because he'd stopped missing her, *needing* her a long time ago.

Because he was falling for another woman. Hard.

He pressed his palms against the wood and levered himself away from the counter. Pulled the chilled champagne out of the wine fridge and started unpeeling the foil. Anything to avoid the truth. That he was terrified of falling so hard again, of putting that power in another person's hands that it was almost blinding.

He worked the cork out of the bottle. The thing was, Izzie wasn't anything like Jess. Sitting across from his ex it had become crystal clear for him. With Izzie, honesty was like a truth serum she'd drunk at birth. Whereas Jess had spun lie after lie, abandoned him when he needed her most, Izzie had given up that story for him. She was strong and she was courageous. And yes, a little neurotic and insecure at the same time. But weren't they all human? Didn't they all have their weaknesses?

The cork hit the ceiling with a resounding thump. The question was, could he offer Izzie more than a brief, few-month affair? Had Jess's betrayal rendered him incapable of trust again?

He picked up the bottle and poured the champagne. His overwhelming instinct was to walk in there and finish what he'd started so she'd call it quits for him. Yet something told him if he messed things up with Izzie, it would be the biggest regret of his life.

Which left him exactly where?

Scooping up the bottle and glasses, he found her on the terrace, looking out at the floodlit 843-acre New York landmark that was Central Park. Her shoulders were straight as a board, her hands curled into fists at her sides.

She turned around. "Alex, I—"

He waved her off. Handed her a glass. "I need to tell you about Jess. About that night…"

Her eyes widened. He walked to the railing, turned and leaned back against it. Started talking before he changed his mind. "I met Jess in high school. She was smart, strong, working two jobs to keep her family going after her mother walked out on them and her dad fell apart and started drinking. I was from a wealthy family. I could help them, so I did. She was determined to keep her brothers and sisters together and not let the family get split up by social services."

"And trying to get through school at the same time," Izzie added quietly. "That must have been tough."

He nodded. "When I finished college and went to play in New York, Jess came to live with me and my sisters. At first things were great. She loved New York, she loved living the life of a professional football player's girlfriend, and I loved indulging her. But then I got injured."

He pulled in a breath at the sudden tightness in his chest. "It's never a good thing when a quarterback tears his rotator cuff, but my physical therapy was going well and there was every indication I'd recover. Jess, on the other hand, wasn't handling it so well. She couldn't handle any kind of uncertainty in her life and the thought of me losing my career made her nuts."

"Because of her past."

He nodded. "She'd heard they were worried about my arm. There was speculation in the press they were grooming Gerry Thompson, the backup quarterback, to take my job. We had a big fight the night before a qualifying game for the playoffs. She said I was being naive. That I didn't see how management was writing me off."

He pulled the top buttons of his shirt open and paced across the terrace. "I went out and had a few too many drinks...wondered if she was right about Gerry."

Izzie pressed her fingers to her temples. "And you decided to play."

He nodded. "I'd been so nervous about my arm and trying to speed my recovery, but I was hurting. A friend told me about this guy who had high-level street painkillers that had helped him through an injury. They worked well, too well for me, and I started to take them regularly, telling myself I could stop when I needed to. That night, when I decided to play, I double dosed. I felt amazing. I was so high by the third quarter I felt invincible. And then I threw that pass."

"I saw the tapes," Izzie said huskily. "It was so perfect."

It had been perfect. It had also been his last. His throat constricted, threatened to cut off the air he so desperately needed. The memory of the ball leaving his hand, sailing through the air in a perfect arc and landing in Xavier's outstretched arms would forever be burned into his mind. The roar of the crowd, the glare of the lights as Xavier dove into the end zone for the touchdown. *He was back.* They were winning. And that was all that had mattered.

The illegal hit, long after the play, had been unexpected. The weight of the defender crashing into him, taking him to the ground until all he could feel was the searing pain in his right arm. *His throwing arm.* The indescribable white-hot burn that had pushed him to his knees. The hush that had fallen over 60,000 fans…the most eerie sound he'd heard in his life.

He blinked hard. The humiliation of being lifted off the field in a stretcher had been the most helpless feeling he'd ever experienced. The knowledge that that night had been the last time he would ever lead his team onto the field excruciating. Because he'd known. *He'd known.*

The weight of Izzie's hand on his forearm brought his gaze up. "There was nothing the doctors could do?"

He shook his head. Each surgeon's diagnosis had been the same. *It's damaged too badly, Alex. Your career is over.*

He ran his fingers through his hair. "I wouldn't go to my father and plead for a job. Jess left me and married Gerry a few months later."

Izzie's fingers tightened around his arm. "She wasn't worth half of you, Alex."

He'd felt as if he wasn't worth anything in those months afterward. His body broken, his future in tatters, it had taken him a year to pull himself together.

He shrugged her fingers off. "I didn't tell you this for your pity. I told you because I need you to understand what happened between Jess and me. I can't be with someone with those types of insecurities."

"How could you not want her back?" She said it as if she couldn't help herself. "She's so stunning. You have so much history together."

"Because I want you," he said quietly. "And if you'd ever stop comparing yourself to that mother and sister of yours, you might actually see why."

A dull red color stained her cheeks. "I know, it's just— hard to break old habits."

"You're going to have to or this isn't going to work." He

stepped closer and ran his thumb over her cheek. "There's a part of me that doesn't believe it has to be the same as it was for our parents.. They made choices. *We* create our own destiny. But, I am only one-half of this equation, Iz. I need you with me."

Her gaze darkened. "I can, I promise you I can. I just may not always be perfect about it. You've got to cut me some slack."

He let out the breath he hadn't even realized he was holding. Hadn't realized how important her answer was to him. He dragged his thumb down over the soft flesh of her bottom lip. "Prove it."

Her eyes widened as she registered what he was asking of her. She pressed her lips shut and took a step backward and he wasn't sure if she was going to run or stay. Then she deposited her glass on the table and moved her fingers to the buttons of her blouse.

She was shaking, her hands fumbling with the tiny pearl buttons. But he held himself back. This had to be all Izzie.

She released the second, the third button; exposed the rounded curves of her breasts. The dusty blue of the silk that encased her flesh made his throat go dry. Down her hands went, dispensing with the rest of the buttons. She pulled the shirt from the waistband of her skirt, shrugged out of it and dropped it to the ground. The dusky imprint of her nipples protruding through the silk made him pull in a breath.

Kill me now. Except he'd asked for this. Some strange, demented part of him needed to see that she had the self-confidence to be with him.

Her hands slid to the zipper of her skirt. She undid it and pushed it down over her hips. Her curves in the almost-there underwear were pure perfection, the dark shadow of her feminine curls drawing his eye. He ached to bury himself in her. *Now.*

Any semblance of self-control vanished. "You can let me know when I'm allowed to put my hands on you," he rasped, his body so hard it was painful. "I'm thoroughly convinced."

She arched a brow at him. "That quick?"

"That quick," he said, taking a step toward her.

She stepped back, giving him a considering look. "I'm not sure I'm done."

He took two steps forward, sank his hands into her waist and slung her over his shoulder. "I am."

The bedroom had been his destination, but his aching body had him diverting to the flat surface of the pool table. He set her down on the edge, stepped between her legs and took her mouth in a kiss that told her this would be no slow seduction. Tonight he needed to take her hard and fast. To exorcise the demons raging in his head.

She moved against him, her low whimper as she wrapped her legs around him and ground the hard ridge of his arousal against her setting his blood on fire. "I can't make this slow tonight," he groaned, burying his face in her throat.

"I don't want it slow," she gasped, clutching his hair. He pressed his mouth to the racing pulse at the base of her throat. Spread her silky thighs with his hand and sought out her slick, wet heat. Her low moan as he sank his middle finger into her almost undid him. When he was sure she was ready, he stepped back, tore at his clothes with his hands. His belt, the button on his pants, his zipper; he didn't stop until he'd freed his rock-hard erection and ripped off the barely there wisps of lace covering her hips. The sight of her wet, glistening flesh as she parted her legs to him was the biggest turn-on he'd ever experienced.

He moved forward, brushed the pulsing, aching length of him against her. She dug her fingers into his forearms. "Please, I need—"

"Look at me."

She opened her eyes, her gaze locking onto his. He reached down and took her hips in his hands, filling her with a thrust that made her gasp and clamp her eyes shut. He paused while her tight body adjusted to him. And when she relaxed, pleaded for more in a desperate, husky voice that made him crazy, he began to move in deep, cathartic strokes that drove everything from his mind but how right it always was with this woman. How easily she made him forget everything but being with her.

The sound of their lovemaking filled the air—the slick push and pull of him sliding into her, the soft little moans she made at the back of her throat when she took him deep, the sound of his raspy breath rapidly losing control…

But still he held back, afraid to unleash that last part of him that took him into the darkness. Afraid of what might happen if he totally lost control.

"Alex," Izzie murmured, watching him. Reading him. "It's okay…please—I want you so much."

His low curse rang out on the night air as he drove into her harder, faster, rougher than he'd ever taken a woman, a primitive part of him reveling in the pain of her fingernails as they dug into the hard flesh of his shoulders. He felt her body tighten around him, clench at him. He slid his fingers under her hips and took more of her weight, arched her higher against him, taking their lovemaking even deeper until he lost himself somewhere along the way. Izzie cried out and convulsed around him, the intense spasms of her body sending him over the edge along with her.

The red-hot pleasure that flashed through him as he came almost brought him to his knees. He held her there, wrapped around him, until his legs felt steady enough to carry her to bed. Then he turned out the lights and they slept.

For the first time in a week he did not dream. There

were no sweat-drenched nightmares of the night every-thing had ended. Sweet, sweet Izzie wrapped around him was like an angel sent to rescue him from a place he could no longer go.

CHAPTER TWELVE

COULD YOUR LIFE actually be this perfect?

Izzie balanced her latte on her knee while James made mincemeat of the entertainment reporter in their morning editorial meeting. And contemplated the question. She was a front-runner for an anchor job currently being hashed out by the execs, she was starting to deal with her insecurities on a fundamental level and she had the man of her dreams at her side to help her do it.

A tiny smile curved her lips. Perhaps it was possible. Maybe Alex was right. Maybe all you had to do was believe it could be different.

She picked up her pen and started doodling as James droned on. It helped to know why Alex was who he was. The demons that haunted him... She knew where she had to bend. When she had to be strong. It was never going to be easy to be with a man like Alex whom everyone wanted a piece of. But she was getting there.

James lit into another reporter, working his way through the room like a raging bull. Izzie put her head down and focused on her doodles. Even her relationship with her mother was showing signs of life. They'd had dinner and coffee a couple of times without actually wanting to tear each other's hair out. And somehow, deep down, it felt as if this time her mother was actually trying. That she wanted to be a part of her life.

She sketched a big question mark on her pad. Opening herself up so completely was life affirming, but it was also terrifying. Because she knew realistically, her mother and Alex could walk away tomorrow and there was nothing she could do about it.

It was a risk she had to take.

"Can someone *please* give me some uplifting news?" James's sarcastically drawled entreaty brought her head up.

"I'll have a rough cut of the Constantinou story ready for you this afternoon," Bart Forsyth piped up. "Right on time."

"A half a day late," her boss ripped back. "How's it going?"

Bart shrugged. "Pretty much ready to go. Messer's refused to do a follow-up interview now that he knows we're positioning Isaacs as the guy behind *Behemoth*. So I'm just polishing it off." He flicked a glance at Izzie. "Did you forget to give me some of your notes?"

She froze, her heart skipping a beat.

"I can't find anything on his Boston College days," Bart continued, frowning. "I thought you said you had that stuff."

Her breath came out in a long whoosh. "Let me check. Maybe I missed something."

James wrapped the meeting up. She was halfway out of her chair when he waved her to a halt. "Give me a minute."

Damn. She hugged her notebook to her chest while the others fled the room. Her heart started to pound. She hadn't done anything to earn a one-on-one berating, had she? *Except bury crucial information.*

Her boss hitched his thigh onto the end of the table and crossed his arms over his chest. "I need you to anchor the news tonight. Gillian's sick."

Her stomach dropped. Anchoring on the weekend was one thing. Anchoring the nightly news, home to multimillions of viewers, was entirely another. "Of course," she made herself respond calmly. "I'd love to."

"It's good timing," he nodded. "The execs are going to make their decision any day. One more chance for you to make an impression."

She forced a bright smile to her lips. "Absolutely."

He went off to unleash his fury on the rest of the staff. Izzie ran clammy palms over her skirt and took a deep breath. She could do this. A bigger audience didn't change anything. And that tricky political panel Gillian hosted every Wednesday night? Maybe they'd have Chris, Gillian's coanchor, do it.

She went back to her desk, dug the notes out for Bart and handed the folder over. Tried to work. But the words blurred on her computer screen and her brain kept bouncing forward to tonight. *Focus. Channel it.*

Another ten minutes went by and she hadn't read a word. She called Alex. He picked up on the third ring, his voice distracted. "What's up?"

She pushed her pencil against her cheek. "You sound busy."

"I'm about to go into a meeting. You okay?"

"Yes, I just—" She stopped as she heard voices in the background. Someone call Alex's name. "It's no biggie. You go. We'll talk later."

"Okay. Look, Iz…" His voice softened. "Jess is having a really rough day and she's asked me for some advice. I'm going to have a drink with her after work, make sure she's okay, then I'll meet you back at the penthouse."

Jealousy clawed at her insides. Weighted down the phone line. "Fine," she said slowly, keeping her voice neutral. "I'm going to be late anyway."

He signed off. She put the phone down and pushed her hands through her hair. *Focus on the things you can control, Iz.* Like tonight.

* * *

When Izzie stepped onto the set that night, her mind was not in the right place. She was jittery, edgy and not on her game. By the time she hosted the political panel on the mayoral race, she was thoroughly shaken by her performance. So was the producer. He started prepping her with cues in her earpiece, but the panel tore her apart, her distraction too great to keep on top of the verbal zings ripping back and forth. They went to break and the producer tried to talk her through it. But it was as if her brain were frozen with fear. As if she were navigating a dark tunnel and couldn't find her way out.

When the red recording light on the camera flicked off, so did what was left of her composure. She unclipped her mic, murmured a robotic thanks to her cohost and walked off the set.

Somehow she found her way to her desk, grabbed her purse and stumbled outside before anyone could approach her. Sucked in the cool night air. She hadn't just been bad. She'd been a complete disaster.

She rode the subway home to her apartment. It felt too small, too claustrophobic after Alex's penthouse, so she yanked on sweats and sneakers and went outside for a run. Her footsteps hit the pavement with a rhythmical *thump, thump* that normally calmed her immediately. Not tonight. She ran down the side streets toward the park as if the devil were on her heels. And thought how amazing it was that life went on as usual when it felt as though yours was falling apart.

Through the park she ran, until her knees threatened to buckle. When she got back to her street, her steps slowed to a walk to cool off. She saw a male figure sitting on the front steps of her brownstone. *Alex.*

"Your boss is worried about you," he said grimly when she stopped in front of him.

She pulled her phone out of her pocket. Three missed calls. "I'll text him. I'm sorry, I didn't mean to alarm you."

He lifted a brow. Banked anger glimmered in his eyes. "I was waiting for you at home."

The hot tears she'd been fighting her entire run slipped down her cheeks. "I'm sorry."

He muttered an oath, stood and gathered her in his arms. "It's okay," he murmured into her hair. "One bad performance isn't going to kill you."

"This one will."

He shook his head. "No one judges you on one performance. You'll do it again. Kill it next time."

"I am not you," she yelled at him, pulling out of his arms with a panicked rage. "I do not thrive on game day. I choke, Alex. *I choked*. There is no way they're giving me another chance."

He frowned. "You don't know that."

"I do." She swiped the tears from her cheeks. "It's done."

His expression softened. "Go get your stuff. We'll talk at my place."

She stood there staring at him, wanting desperately to run into his arms and have him make everything right. But she was afraid to want him that much. To *need* him that much.

She lifted her chin. "I think I should stay here tonight."

"Why?" His response was low and shot through with challenge.

She looked away. "I just think it's a good idea given everything that's happened tonight."

Antagonism flared in his eyes. "You think something happened between Jess and me?"

"No…" She shook her head, but his penetrating gaze read her uncertainty.

"*Christós,* Izzie." He clenched his hands by his sides. "I was home worried sick about you, terrified something might have happened, when it finally occurred to me you might be here. I drive over here like a maniac, putting the lives of myself and others in danger, you're not here, and I'm dying." Fury shimmered in his eyes. "So don't act like you don't trust me when I'm obviously crazy about you."

Her heart slammed against her chest. *Crazy about her?* "I'm not doubting you," she summoned haltingly. "I just—"

"Exactly," he muttered. "You just are."

"Can you not see what she's doing?" she burst out. "She keeps asking for your help because she wants you back."

"And you need to trust me. That's what relationships are all about, Iz. Trusting the person you're with."

She locked her gaze with his. "Tell me she doesn't want you back, Alex."

Ruddy color dusted his cheekbones. "I've told you she means nothing to me anymore."

"Then tell her to find another shoulder to cry on," Izzie challenged.

"Because you can't *handle* it? I thought we'd been through this. You need to grow up."

She gave him a belligerent look. "Maybe you do, too, because that woman is only interested in one thing. *You.*"

A thunderous cloud fell over his face. "You're just about succeeding, you know that, Iz?"

She arched a brow at him. "Succeeding in what?"

"Pushing me away." He took a step toward her, picked her up and stalked to his car.

"What are you doing?" she demanded in a voice this side of shrill.

"Watching over you so you don't self-destruct," he muttered, tossing her in the car and demanding her keys. "Call your boss," he ordered. Then he marched up to her apartment, retrieved her purse and computer, slid back into the car, and drove her to his place.

Brushing aside her usual request to walk the twenty flights up to his penthouse with a roll of his eyes, he hustled her into the elevator. She sat numbly on the sofa while he made her an omelet, forced her to eat it, then put her under a hot shower. When she'd taken up second residence there, he ordered her out and to bed. She went willingly because her head was pounding, her body spent, and all she wanted to do was pretend this day had never happened.

Alex brought his laptop to bed and tucked her against his side while he worked. She burrowed into him, desperate for his warmth, for his ability to make everything better.

"I backslid badly today," she murmured. "I know it."

He brushed her hair away from her face, his expression softening. "I'll cut you some slack tonight."

"You're really crazy about me?"

His mouth tilted. "Unfortunately since I don't think you're going to make this easy on me, yes."

She curved her hand around his thigh. He gave her a wary look. "You need sleep, Iz."

"I need you," she corrected huskily, closing her fingers over the thick, hard length of him.

"Iz…"

She slid her hand inside his boxers and found his velvet heat. He ditched the laptop then. Flipped her over and started to explore her bare skin from the top down. "Does this feel like my interest is anywhere but right here?" he demanded, imprinting her with his considerable male assets.

"No," she gasped. But she let him prove it in a no-holds-barred exhibition of how he could make her forget her name. Down, down she went into the maelstrom that was Alex. Handed over that last piece of her heart she'd been holding back because if he wanted her like this, in her worst train-wreck moment of all time, she was already long, long gone. Had been, she feared, from that first night in London.

CHAPTER THIRTEEN

ALEX LEFT AT 5:30 a.m. to fly to Seattle after making her promise not to do anything rash. To think this through and talk to James before she drew any conclusions. She made the promise, slunk back into bed and slept for another couple of hours. Then she stumbled into Alex's big, bright walk-in steam shower and thought about putting her life back together.

She was obeying the eye-opening prompt of the eucalyptus body wash he favored when the bottle dropped from her fingers.

The notes.

Scenes from the night before flashed through her head. Her removing the Taylor Johnson transcript from Alex's file before handing it to Bart Forsyth. The scan through she'd done to make sure all other evidence of the illegal painkillers was removed. Her stomach lurched. What she had forgotten was the original set of notes from her interview with Taylor tucked in the front pocket.

She'd given Bart the evidence on the drugs.

Oh my God.

She fled the shower, threw on her pants from the night before and a spare shirt she kept in Alex's closet, then cabbed it to the station. It was quiet at eight-thirty, with only a few reporters at their desks. A frantic, covert search of Bart's desk for the folder was unsuccessful. She sat down at her own, rested her head in her shaking hands and drew in deep breaths. Bart either had the file at home with him, which meant he might have read it last night, or he'd locked it in his drawer.

Either way, she was in trouble. Her guts churned in sickening recognition of how much trouble. *Everything*, her job, Alex's reputation, was on the line if those interview notes were discovered. How could she have done it? Sure, she'd been stressed, but this was inconceivable.

She sat there, frozen to the spot, pretending to work until Bart came in an hour later. He gave her his usual whack on the shoulder and went off whistling to the kitchen to get his coffee. She rose and flew to his desk. There on the top was the blue folder. Heart slamming in her chest, she flicked it open, grabbed the notes and committed the most unrecoverable sin of her career. She hurried back to her desk and buried them in her purse for destruction at a later date. And hoped, *prayed* fate was on her side. Bart hadn't said anything about the notes, and surely he would have if he'd read such explosive testimony?

Maybe she'd slipped by by the skin of her teeth...

A fine sheen of perspiration broke out on her brow. James came in and she suffered through a horrendous debriefing of her performance the night before, during which he confirmed that she had indeed done her chances at the anchor job a great deal of damage. But he wouldn't know how much until he talked with management. Meanwhile, he told her, stay the course. Pull yourself together and see what happens.

She was only too happy to put her head down and do her job, but by the end of the day, her nerves were frayed beyond repair. Neither Bart nor James had said anything, she had no idea if they knew about Taylor Johnson or not, and she could barely prevent herself from lurching to the bathroom and throwing up what little lunch she'd consumed.

She was packing up her stuff when her phone buzzed. She looked down at it. *A reminder of dinner with her mother.* Oh God no. She could not do that tonight. She could not. Unfortunately, her mother didn't pick up when she called to cancel and was likely on her way to the restaurant.

Her mother had a bottle of Chianti on the table when she arrived at the elegant little Italian trattoria on Fifth Avenue that treated its Hollywood clientele with an understated attention to detail Dayla loved. Her mother gave her a long look, rose and kissed her on the cheek.

"We're drinking."

Izzie collapsed in the leather chair opposite her mother. "I might need more than a bottle."

Her mother gestured for the waiter to pour her some wine. "What happened?"

The same as before...except this time she'd fallen apart in front of millions of viewers.

Her mother sighed. "Everyone has bad performances, Izzie. Pick yourself up and move on."

"Maybe you were right that day in L.A." She fixed her mother with a belligerent stare. "Maybe I'm just not cut out for the spotlight."

Her mother took a sip of her wine and set it down. "What do you think?"

"I don't know," she returned in an antagonized tone. "I like being in front of the camera when I'm out on assignment. Anchoring...that's a whole other story."

Her mother sat back in her chair. "You don't thrive in the spotlight like your sister and I do. And you don't have the same thick skin. You thought I was being unnecessarily cruel guiding you away from acting, but I was trying to protect you, Izzie. The pressure to be always on, to always look perfect...to never be able to escape the public eye no matter how much you want to." She shook her head.

"It's unrelenting. I may have been a terrible mother, but I never wanted you to go through that. You're too smart. You have too much to give. Look at those stories you do out in the community. You were always one of those kids who was going to change the world." She gave her a penetrating look. "Maybe that's all you need."

Izzie stared at her, stunned into silence.

"If you get that anchor job," her mother continued, "it's always going to be about how good you look for how long. A glorified popularity contest. A political tug-of-war that will never end. Sure you can affect change in that role, you'll have the power, but it isn't going to be about the story anymore. It's going to be about your image."

Izzie twisted her hands in her lap, wondering where *this* mother had been all her life. "I don't even know if I want the job...or if it's even a possibility anymore."

Her mother frowned. "So why kill yourself trying to win a job that stresses you out this much?"

Because I've never stopped trying to win your approval. Because despite the fact that I told myself I didn't care what you thought anymore, I've spent my entire career trying to prove I'm good enough for you.

She blinked back the tears that threatened. Her mother reached across the table and wrapped her fingers around hers. "Live with it for a day or two, Iz. You'll know what the right decision is."

Izzie stared down at her mother's hand wrapped around hers and felt her chest constrict. "I can't have you walking in and out of my life," she said heavily. "It's too hard."

Her mother's fingers tightened around hers. "I'm not going anywhere. I promise you that, Iz. Not anymore."

Izzie's phone beeped. Releasing her mother's hand, she dug it out and saw that the message was from Alex. He had sent her another one of his quotes. Courage was not the absence of fear, but the triumph over it. Nelson Mandela. How are you?

Her mouth curved.

"Alex?" her mother asked.

"Yes."

Her mother's gaze sharpened on her. "You're crazy about him."

Her smile faded. "Yes."

"So why don't you look happier?"

She picked up a piece of bread and buttered it with elaborate precision. "We argued last night."

"About?"

"His ex-girlfriend." She abandoned any pretense of eating and laid the bread on her side plate. "His stunning ex-girlfriend he almost married who wants him back."

Her mother gave her a long look. "Do you trust him?"

"Yes."

"Then what's the problem?"

"I don't trust myself." She'd proven that last night, hadn't she? Her insecurities had cost her an anchor job and made Alex doubt her. Again.

"Maybe you should figure out why," her mother said softly. "It's clear you're madly in love with him, Iz."

She swallowed past the huge lump in her throat. "What if I'm not enough? What if he decides he's still in love with her?"

Her mother's mouth twisted. "Life is all about the chances we take. You can't reap the rewards if you don't put yourself out there."

And hadn't that night in London taught her that? Why was she having this huge regression? Was she determined to be a self-fulfilling prophecy? Or was her direction all wrong?

Her mother took a sip of wine and set it down. "You know how I remember you as a child? You were always the little daredevil, jumping off walls, falling off the balance beam, wild for roller coasters..." A smile lit her eyes. "Wild for trouble. You used to give us heart attacks. I swear I took you to the emergency room so many times when you were around six or seven they started to look at me funny."

Izzie smiled. "My right elbow still aches on rainy days."

"The monkey bar break." Her mother looked down at her wineglass and twisted the crystal stem between her fingers. "I remember talking to your father after I left, checking in on you guys. He told me Ella was her usual 'I don't care about anything' self, and that you were fine, doing great at school and raking in a bunch of athletic awards. But he knew you were hurting." She looked up at her daughter. "Then he said something that made me very sad."

Izzie felt her composure slipping, the memory of those awful first months trying to keep it all together, ones she never let herself revisit. Her mother's eyes grew suspiciously bright. "He said he'd been talking to your swimming coach about your progress and your coach had said it was a shame you didn't take risks anymore because you were good, but you could have been great."

Izzie drew in a breath, feeling as if she'd just been socked in the stomach. She dropped her gaze and found herself staring at her mother's shaking hands. *Please not now.* She couldn't do this now.

"What happened between your father and me was complex, Izzie." Her mother's voice held a lifetime of regret. "I know you think I destroyed him, but it's not that simple. Life isn't that simple. And not everyone's going to walk out on you. I promise you that. Take a chance on Alex. He seems like he's worth it."

Izzie thought about herself as that daredevil little girl. How that part of her had come out that night in London.

And wondered if she could channel it again. Because her mother was right. Alex *was* worth it. And she was madly, head-over-heels in love with him.

Alex leaned back against the elevator wall, his mouth curving. It seemed like forever ago he'd gotten stuck in that elevator with the whirling dervish who'd transformed his life, but in reality it had only been six weeks. Six weeks to him finding his penthouse empty without her. Six weeks to the man who never entertained the concept of long-term doing it on a regular basis.

He'd had plenty of time to think on his whirlwind twenty-four-hour trip to Seattle. And he'd come to the realization that Izzie had been right about Jess. He'd been so busy being self-righteous, he hadn't stopped to think how he would have felt if it had been her out to dinner with an ex she'd once been crazy about. No, he'd never given her any reason to doubt him, and she should trust him. But his ex did want him back. And that was different. He needed to tell Jess to find someone else to support her. He couldn't be that person. Not anymore.

He watched the skyline of Manhattan fly by as the glass-walled elevator slid upward. His need to prove himself to his father was the root cause of his biggest failures. The question was, could he alter that pattern for the future? Could he avoid being a chip off the old block in all the ways that mattered?

The doors opened on the fiftieth floor. He was so lost in thought it took him three tries to punch in the security code that bypassed the receptionist's desk through the back doors. There wasn't one minute since he'd met Isabel Peters that he hadn't known she was different. She made him a little insane—yes. But he was also starting to think she might be the one. That he might be in love with her.

His hand froze on the handle of the double glass doors

that led to the executive offices. He'd sworn he'd never utter those words again after Jess had left. Did he have it in him to be the man who stayed when Izzie seemed to want to run every time things got tough?

He thought, perhaps, yes.

Head spinning, he pushed through the doors and headed toward Grace to grab his messages. Tonight, according to the heads-up James Curry had given him, Frank Messer's accusations were going to die a slow death in front of America. Sophoros would finally be rid of him with the generous settlement Alex had put together to make Messer disappear *forever* this time, and things would be back to normal. *Then* he would deal with Izzie.

Mark was sitting on Grace's desk, which wasn't an unusual sight per se, but the dark look on his face was. "Alex," Grace greeted him, getting jerkily to her feet. "You're back."

His PA's face was pale, her hands flailing uselessly at her sides. His smile faded. "What's wrong?"

Grace's gaze darted to Mark, then back to him. "Izzie's been trying to reach you."

He fished his phone out of his pocket. It was still on airplane mode. He'd missed *five* calls from Izzie?

An uneasy feeling snaked up his spine. "Is she okay?"

"Yes, I think so—she—" His assistant darted another glance at Mark. "I told her you were on your way. She's coming over."

His gaze narrowed. "What is going on, you two?"

"NYC-TV just ran the preview of your story," Mark said quietly.

The hairs on the back of his neck stood up. "Curry told me the story sided with Sophoros…"

"I think they went in a dif—"

His name blared from the television. A picture of him in a New York Crusaders uniform flashed across the screen.

A headline ran in the ticker beneath it. Painkiller Addiction Destroyed Football Hero's Career.

Blood whooshed in his ears. His legs went weak. He clutched the side of Grace's desk and stared at the screen. *This couldn't be happening.* Izzie had buried that information.

A clip of his old teammate Taylor Johnson flashed up on the screen. The host previewed an exclusive interview with him that evening: an athlete from the inside on how drugs were destroying professional sports. His blood ran cold. How could Johnson know? He hadn't been in the locker room that night. Xavier had been the only one with him, telling him not to do it.

A mad feeling of unreality enveloped him. *This was impossible.*

The host moved on to preview the weather. Alex stared at the screen, hands clenched at his sides, fighting the urge to tear the television from the wall. The clatter of high heels tapping across the tile floor brought his head around. Izzie half ran the last few steps down the hallway. He took one look at her panicked expression and pointed at his office. "Go."

She put her head down and did as she was told. He sucked in a lungful of air, walked into his office and slammed the door. She jumped, her hand flying to her mouth.

"What the hell," he bit out, "was that? Xavier and I were the only ones in the locker room that night."

"Taylor said he saw you take the drugs." Her voice was low but steady. "He knew the dealer. Had an issue himself."

His insides felt as though they were on fire. "Who told Bart about this?"

The color drained from her face. "I didn't mean to, Alex. I gave him some notes and—"

"I don't care how," he roared. "Did you or did you not

give Bart Forsyth the information about the illegal pain-killers?"

"Yes," she choked out. "But I didn't mean to. I—"

"Stop," he thundered. *"Stop."*

He stood there, legs spread apart, her answer tearing him to pieces. He'd been dying, *begging* for her to say no, she hadn't done it. But she had.

"That's all I need to know." His voice was so low, hollow-sounding, he didn't even recognize it as his own. "Get out."

"Alex, please, you have to listen to me."

He shook his head. "That's been my stupidity all along, Iz. I did listen to you. I believed in you. And you were just playing me for a fool." A muscle jumped in his jaw. "What do they say, 'fool me once, shame on you; fool me twice, shame on me.'"

"Alex, no. I—"

He threw up a hand and stalked to the door, twisted the handle, and threw it open before he said or did something unforgivable. "Get out of my life, Izzie."

She didn't move. Just stood there staring at him, her face paper-white. She was a really good actress, he decided. How had he not figured that out?

"I'm so sorry," she said finally, as if she knew nothing she said could make it better. "I swear I never meant to hurt you."

He hardened his heart against the tears shimmering in those beautiful eyes of hers. "The cameras aren't running, Iz. You can turn off the waterworks."

Grace gasped behind her. He waited until Izzie had walked out, then slammed the door. If he never saw Isabel Peters again, it would be too soon.

CHAPTER FOURTEEN

IZZIE OPERATED LIKE a robot for days. She forced herself out of bed, into the shower, onto the subway and to work, but she was functioning at half capacity, if that. She ate when she remembered to, which wasn't often, she slept through an entire weekend and didn't bother to work out. Not even her girlfriends' attempts to get her out for a drink were successful. She felt like wallowing in her misery, so that's exactly what she did.

Her first day back to work after Alex's story aired, James called her into his office. He had been acting as though he hadn't known about the drugs, he'd said, so he and Bart could get the story to air without her tipping off Alex and his lawyers. But it didn't mean he wasn't furious. She'd never seen him so angry. He could hardly speak to her. So he banished her to her desk, told her to keep her head down, and he'd figure out her punishment. Which may or may not include firing her. The execs still hadn't made up their minds about an anchor and he wasn't sure he could support her even if they chose her.

She was happy to put her head down and focus on her job, because it allowed her not to think about the mess she'd made of her relationship with the man she loved and gave her a chance to think about the future. To think about what she really wanted. Because she'd spent too much time with her eye on a prize she wasn't sure was even for her.

Her mother came over one night with two bottles of wine, and they drank one each. It was, it seemed, the only part of her life that was going in the right direction.

A couple of weeks into her exile, James called her into his office. It was the first time he'd spoken to her one-on-one since that conversation about her future. She walked in, palms sweaty, heart hammering in her chest. *Please, God. Don't fire me.*

He looked up from his schedule and waved her into the chair opposite him. "You remember the story Bart did on the River City Collegiate Warriors—the high school football team that'd been pegged for the state finals this year until they lost their coach in the big accident on the turnpike?"

She nodded. It was a hard story to forget.

"They've been struggling, but they still have a chance at state. I want you to go out and do a follow-up story on them. Put together a nice rah-rah piece that makes everyone feel good."

She sat up. "James—"

His mouth hardened. "I'm giving you a second chance, Iz. Get out of my office and prove to me you're the professional I know you are."

She got jerkily to her feet. *He wasn't going to fire her. She was going to keep her job.* The fog that had enveloped her brain these past few weeks lifted as she made her way to her desk. She had a chance to turn this around. So football was Alex. So it might break her heart to do this. She needed to put her feelings aside and act like a professional. James was right. She might not know if she wanted that anchor job, but she did love her current one. And she was going to knock this story out of the park.

She went to the River City practice that afternoon. It

was impossible not to watch the tough young quarterback trying to rally a team that had lost its heart and not think of Alex. Of how terrifying it must have been for him to walk out onto that field that night knowing his career was hanging in the balance. How she, who'd wanted to be the one to prove to him he could trust again, had been the one to destroy him.

The ball of hurt that had permanently lodged itself in her chest expanded, making it hard to breathe. If she learned nothing else from this heartbreak, she needed to learn she was *enough*. Because that was all she had.

She pulled in a deep breath, waiting for the oxygen to remind her a broken heart couldn't actually physically hurt her. That someday she would get over Alex and move on. Because it *was* over. She hadn't heard from him since that awful scene in his office when he'd looked at her as if he hated her. She was pretty sure he did.

Her eyes blurred as she watched the quarterback throw a bullet down the field for a touchdown. His teammates swarmed around him, slapping him on the back. They were regrouping. It was time she did too.

Jim Carter, the River City assistant coach in charge of the team until they found a head coach replacement, waved at her to join them on the field. She plastered a smile on her face and went down. Carter, a harassed-looking guy in his early forties, flashed her a distracted smile. "Sorry 'bout that. We're still a little all over the place without a head coach."

Izzie frowned. "I heard there were lots of candidates."

"Haven't found the right fit. We're lookin' for someone with Division One experience, and that ain't easy to find."

Alex had Division One experience. She bit her lip. "Would you take someone part-time? Someone with a great deal of experience to help out?"

Carter hooked his thumbs into his belt loops. "Who were you thinking of?"

She pursed her lips. A team that needed a hero. A man who needed to be a hero again... During their time together, she'd seen how much it had hurt Alex to exile himself from football. Had seen the hollow look in his eyes every time she accidentally flicked on a game on the television. She twisted her ponytail, thinking hard. Would Alex even consider it? His schedule was nuts, yes, but word had it the Messer case was being settled out of court.

She gave Carter an even look. "Give Alex Constantinou a call."

His brow furrowed. "The way I heard it, the guy wants nothin' to do with football."

"Call him," she said firmly. "I think he might feel differently if he meets the team."

"And you know this how?"

A sharp pang sliced through her. "I know Alex," she said quietly. "Give it a shot."

When Jim Carter called her two days later to say Alex had agreed to stop by a practice, it was a bittersweet moment. Maybe something, *something* good would come out of all of this.

"Jim, don't tell him I had anything to do with this, okay?"

He sounded curious, but agreed. She hung up. Walked into James's office and took herself out of the running for the anchor job. And felt as if the weight of the world had been lifted off her shoulders.

The smell of fresh-cut grass hit Alex first. The earthy, pungent fragrance of the dirt underneath, turned up by the players' cleats, came next. They were smells he could have conjured just by closing his eyes. Recalling the hundreds of times he'd walked out onto a field just like this. But today as he did it for the first time in eight years, he knew why he'd never come back.

It felt as though someone was tearing his heart out.

Shoving his hands in his pockets, he climbed the bleachers. He would stay for a half hour to make Carter happy. Then he'd tell him he couldn't do it and leave. Because he couldn't.

He leaned his forearms on the railing of the first row and watched Carter put the team through drills. The players reminded him of the torn-up, patchy-looking field. They'd seen better days. But there was talent here. Lots of it. Belief was the issue. Vision.

His mouth twisted. He knew the feeling. In the weeks following the airing of his feature, his office had been flooded with phone calls from media outlets wanting a piece of him. Desperate for a new angle, desperate to get a piece of a story that was captivating the airwaves. Were athletes pushing it too far with drugs? Was the pressure on them too great?

He flexed his arms and pushed away from the railing. His faith in humanity had taken a beating. He'd gone underground, avoided the calls that came daily from his three sisters. Told Mark to mind his own business. Then his sisters had shown up at his office and dragged him out for a talking-to. "It's better that it's all out," Agape, the pragmatist, had said. "Now you can move on."

Surprisingly, she'd been right. He felt a strange sense of freedom in no longer having anything to hide. To put a period on a part of his life that was over. So what was he doing here dredging it up all over again? "Just come meet the team," Carter had said. "Take in a practice. If you're still not interested, no harm done."

Carter yelled some instructions to the offensive line

and hopped up into the bleachers beside him. "What do you think?"

He shrugged. "Lots of talent out there."

Carter nodded, slid him a sideways look. "They need a leader."

"That wouldn't be me." Alex kept his eyes on the field. "I haven't played football in eight years."

"I'd say it'd be a right fresh start for you then."

He stared at the field, at the crooked uprights, at the sport that was everything he'd once loved. Why the hell wasn't he telling Carter no? Getting out of here?

Because in the wake of his disillusionment over Frank Messer, walking out onto this field today had been the rightest thing he'd done in a long, long time. He needed to believe again. And this team had an amazing story.

He looked at the scrappy young quarterback out there. So full of promise. So full of doubt. And knew he could help him.

He looked over at Carter. "I have an insane travel schedule."

"We'll work around it." A wide grin split the coach's face. "You in?"

"Guess I am."

Alex spent every minute of his spare time working with the team over the next couple of weeks. He devoted one-on-one time to every player, finding out what made them tick. What would make them gel as a unit. And finally, he started to see some cohesion. Some of that old brilliance shine through. He pulled in some favors, took them on a field trip to see the New York Crusaders play, hoping the glitz and excitement of watching a pro game in a private box would fire them up.

And somewhere along the way, felt himself heal.

He worked until he was bone-weary at night, then he came home and strategized. Built his game book. But no matter how tired he got, no matter how much he told himself it was a good thing Izzie was out of his life after what she'd done to him, she was everywhere. In his head, in his bed when he finally gave in and crashed at night, on the sofa watching him work, reading his copy of *Great Expectations* and interrupting him to debate the merits of the book.

It was a problem.

A few days before the game that would determine whether the Warriors went to state, he came home late, took a long, hot shower and headed out to the terrace, a beer in his hand. He opened his playbook, started to scribble some notes from today's practice, then stopped. There was one thing, *one thing* he couldn't figure out. If Izzie had intended to betray him all along, why hadn't she kept the story for herself and taken all the credit? Lynched him and guaranteed herself the anchor job?

It didn't make sense. That story had made Bart Forsyth a household name.

He dropped his head in his hands. *I didn't mean to*, she'd said in his office. He'd been so angry, so blind with fury he hadn't been able to see past anything but the fact that she'd splashed his deepest humiliation across the national news. But now, now that he could actually think, he realized he'd done exactly the same thing he'd done to her in the beginning. He'd judged her without letting her explain. Convicted her without a trial instead of believing in the woman he knew she was.

He was afraid he'd made a horrendous mistake.

He picked up the phone and called James Curry. When he was done he felt ill. All that talk he'd fed Izzie about believing in him. When he was the biggest fool of all.

He'd thrown a Hail Mary pass to win that championship for Boston College, its first in too many years to count. A desperate, adrenaline-fueled prayer that had somehow come out right. Could he do it again with the woman who'd captured his heart?

CHAPTER FIFTEEN

THE NIGHT THE River City Warriors took the field in their first game at home with their new assistant coach, Alexios Constantinou—a berth in the state championship at stake—the crisp fall evening, clear and crackling with tension, was the kind that had new beginnings written all over it.

Jim Carter had stepped back and let Alex lead. The players clearly respected, *idolized* him. And he had pushed them hard. He'd demanded they grieve, honor their fallen mentor, then move on. Focus. And in doing so he'd found his own kind of peace. But as he finished his pregame pep talk and sent the players out onto the field, a frozen tension gripped his body. He could hear the roar of the crowd from the tunnel. Knew there were hundreds of people out there to watch the Warriors play. And just as many to witness his return to football.

The buzz was immense. For the second time in his life, he could feel the pressure of a whole city's pride winding its way around his throat, choking him.

"That's a different team goin' out there tonight," Jim Carter said quietly at his side.

Alex nodded. Because he could not speak.

"Ready?"

He started walking by way of reply, down the tunnel toward the field. The lights blinded him as he stepped outside. The noise swept over him like an untamed beast. He blinked as the past and present collided like the cold and hot air of a viciously powerful storm. And found he couldn't move.

Eight years slid away. Suddenly the field was so quiet you could hear a pin drop. The voices of his teammates echoed in his head, reassuring him as they carried him off the field on a stretcher. "*You're gonna be all right, Consty. Hang in there.*"

But it hadn't been all right. It had been over.

The chanting started then, low at first, then louder. He lifted his head.

"*Alllexx, Alllexx, Alllexx.*"

They were chanting his name.

"Check out the signs," Carter said.

He lifted his gaze to the big handmade poster boards littering the crowd.

The Bull Is Back

Welcome Back #45

We Love You Alexios

His throat seized. *How was he supposed to do this?*

Carter gave him a sideways look. Somehow he started moving, putting one foot in front of the other until it became an unconscious rhythm that carried him to the bench. *Focus*, he told himself, the lump in his throat so large he could hardly swallow. *Channel it. You have a job to do.*

That was when he saw her. Seated in the press section of the bleachers, Izzie looked beautiful in a soft blue dress, her hair loose around her shoulders.

She was fumbling—with her purse, with her notebook, looking anywhere but at the Warriors' bench. He clenched his hands at his sides. He'd gone into the station to find her on Monday only to be told she was in the Caribbean for a long weekend with her sister.

Her gaze flicked to him now, as if she couldn't help herself, as if she knew he was watching her. She had stayed away from every practice he'd been around for. Avoided him completely. And she didn't look good. Didn't look rested. She looked pale and thinner than he'd ever seen her.

Carter nudged him. "They're ready for the coin toss."

He nodded. Dragged his gaze away.

"You know she was the one who told me to call you."

"Who?"

"Izzie."

"Izzie?"

Carter nodded. "She asked me not to say anything. But I'm thinkin' you might want to know that."

His heart flipped over with an emotion he hadn't felt in many, many years. *She had known he needed this. Needed football back in his life.* And he wondered how he could ever have let the most courageous woman he knew go.

Carter nudged him. "We gotta go."

He put his head down and walked to the center of the field.

Izzie had been on edge the entire game, but with the Warriors down by one point with three seconds left, she was practically hyperventilating. The Warriors kicker lined up for the field goal, the lights glinting off his dark hair. If he made it, the Warriors went to state. If he missed it, they were out.

After spending weeks working on this story, getting to know each one of these players' personal histories—what they'd gone through—she *needed* for them to win.

Her gaze flicked to Alex, standing motionless on the sidelines. His feet were spread wide, his eyes glued to the kicker as one of the special teams players placed the ball on the tee. To see him in his element, to see how alive his face was, made her heart throb in her chest.

The kicker backed up, eyed the ball, then ran forward

and sent it flying through the air. She craned her neck, tracking the ball as it soared through the glare of the lights and headed for the uprights. It had the height, but it was veering to the right. Her breath caught in her throat. She angled her body to the left, willing it to straighten out. And almost as if it was obeying her command, the ball scraped through the upright by inches.

The crowd erupted. Somehow this bedraggled, courageous team had done the impossible.

The bench emptied as the clock ran out, the players heaping themselves on top of one another in a tangle of red jerseys at midfield. Alex remained where he was, hands planted on his hips, a solitary figure among the mayhem. The lump in her throat grew to gargantuan proportions. And something inside her became unhinged.

If only she hadn't been so stupid.

Nick, her cameraman, stood and nodded toward the scrum of reporters forming around Alex.

"Ready?"

No. But she forced herself to nod and follow Nick down to the field. "Start with Alex?" he suggested.

She shook her head. "Let's start with Danny."

She managed to force half a dozen wooden questions out of her mouth, which the beaming young quarterback attempted to answer around his teammates' whoops and back slaps. The fact that Alex was giving an interview to a *Times* reporter a couple of yards away didn't help. The ache in her chest increased until she felt that her heart would throb out of it. She took a step backward, wrapped her arms around herself and declared the interview done.

Nick started to move toward Alex.

"No."

He stared at her as she pulled her microphone off. "What do you mean no? We need a sound bite from Alex."

"I can't do it."

"What happened to the most courageous woman I know? You can't ask me a few questions?"

She spun around at the sound of Alex's deep, rich voice. His gaze burned into her, all hot blue intensity. "I'm ready."

"Awesome, let's do it." Nick moved forward and refastened her mic with a let's-get-this-over-with look on his face. She took a deep breath, willing some air into her lungs. *What was Alex doing?*

Nick secured a mic to Alex's shirt and stepped back to turn the camera on. The other reporters watched from the sidelines, waiting for their turn. Izzie's tongue was stuck to the roof of her mouth, her brain incapable of constructing a question.

"How did it feel out there tonight?" Nick hissed from behind her.

She blurted the question out.

Alex smiled, his relaxed half smile that made her toes curl. "It felt great. Really really great. I'd forgotten how much I love this game."

Silence.

"What did you think of the team tonight?" Nick prompted.

Izzie asked the question.

"They were everything I knew they could be. The talent was there, they just needed to believe in themselves."

"You're a former quarterback," she said, her brain kicking in. "What did you think of Danny out there?"

Anyone else would have missed the flicker of emotion in that dark blue gaze. The pain he couldn't quite hide. "He's going to be a force to be reckoned with. He directed that team tonight like a true leader. I could see him playing pro ball someday."

"And what do you think about your chances at state?"

"I think we'll take it one day at a time."

And that was a perfect ending. "Well, that's great," she

concluded, plastering a smile across her face. "Congratulations and thank you v—"

"Aren't you going to ask me what lessons *I've* learned?"

Her heart skipped a beat. No—no she wasn't. She reached for her mic, but Alex kept talking, his gaze pinning her to the spot. "I've learned from this team that the past is the past and at some point we all have to move on. That trust is imperative, yet even when we know that, sometimes we still manage to screw up."

This wasn't about football. "Alex…"

"I'm not done."

Two dozen sets of eyes latched onto them, the press scrum clueing in to a whole other story entirely. She yanked off her mic. "I think we are."

"I know you didn't mean to hand over those notes, Iz."

She froze, mic in hand. He took a step closer, until they were only inches apart. "James told me what happened. I'm so sorry. Here I was preaching trust, when I wasn't trusting you at all."

Confusion rained down over her, making her head spin. He *believed* her? She flicked a glance at the reporters surrounding them. "I'm not sure this is the time or pl—"

"I don't give a crap where we are," he growled. "I want to know what happened."

She pulled in a breath. "The night I filled in as the weekday anchor, I was stressed—it was so last-minute. I owed Bart some notes, so I took the file over to him, but I was so distracted, I forgot about my backup notes from Taylor's interview." The ache in her throat had her swallowing hard. "It was a mistake. I— I swear to God I never meant to hurt you."

"I know." He pulled off his mic and handed it to Nick. "I was so angry at first, I couldn't see straight. Having my past splashed across the nation, thinking you'd betrayed me. It was too much. Then, later when my mind cleared, none of it made any sense. Why would you give up the story if you were going to betray me? If it was all about your ambition..."

She felt whatever composure she had left start to crumble. "I turned the job down."

"You did *what*?"

"I'm learning to trust myself. I thought about what I really wanted. And funnily enough, I just want to do my job. I want to go out there every day and tell stories about the soup kitchen lady who feeds the neighborhood out of her own pocket every night. Or Joey the mutt who catches purse snatchers..." She turned to Nick. "Can you please stop filming?"

"Not on your life."

She cursed under her breath. "Where are you going with all this?" she asked Alex. "I know you hate me. You'll always hate me for putting you through that."

He slid his fingers under her chin and held her gaze captive. "I'm asking for your forgiveness," he said softly. "Everything you've ever done has been for me, Iz. From giving up that story, to burying the truth, to getting me back on this football field tonight. You are courage personified. But instead of seeing that, I let my trust issues get in the way. And I am sorry. So sorry."

Her heart melted. Along with her knees. *What was he trying to say?*

A fierce glint entered his eyes. "I want you back...and this time I'm not letting you go."

Her stomach dropped out of her. The tears that had been threatening rolled down her cheeks. "Alex—"

He ran his thumbs across her cheeks and wiped the tears away. "Why are you crying?"

"Because you're on a football field," she burst out, unable to hold it together any longer. "And you look so happy.

The team's won and everything's right with the world. How could I feel anything else when I—"

His mouth tipped up at the corners. He slid his fingers to her jaw and cradled her face in his hands. "Finish the sentence, Iz."

Her mind went full circle. Back to that night in London when a big risk had led her to him. To thinking that no other man would ever live up to him. Finding out she'd been right. And being sure she'd lost him for good. She knew who she was now. And even though she might not be perfect, even though she might screw up many more times in her life, she really didn't want to live with regrets.

"All right," she said, looking up at him. "I was going to say I love you. That I—"

His kiss, fierce and hard, silenced her. He kissed her until her arms wound their way around his neck, and she didn't care if the entire press corps, the *entire world* was watching, which they might be later since Nick was still filming.

Alex pulled back. "I've told Jess she needs to find someone else to talk to. I should have been more considerate of your feelings given my history with her."

She bit her lip. "I have to let it go. I know that. I won't ever be perfect but I know I can do better."

He shifted his weight to the other foot, the strangest look coming over his face.

"What's wrong? I promise I'll do better."

He dropped to one knee.

"You aren't actually doing this to me, are you?" she asked faintly.

He grinned. "You'd better believe it, sweetheart. And I'm sweating bullets right now, so stay with me."

Her heart beat like a jackhammer. Sped even faster when he reached into his jacket and took out a tiny box.

"You have a ring," she croaked.

His mouth twitched. "Brilliant deduction. Just one of the things I love about you—your incredibly sharp brain. Followed closely by your slight neuroticism, your incurable love of those trashy romance novels, your insatiable need for control and even the way you eat your food, which, by the way, I do think is very odd, but I love it anyway."

The tears started up again, sliding down her cheeks like runaway bandits.

"But what I love most about you," he added softly, his gaze holding hers, "is your courage. Because you are the most courageous woman I know, Isabel Peters."

The stream of tears turned into a flood.

He flipped opened the box to reveal a stunning square-cut pink diamond, surrounded by a row of sparkling white stones. He looked up at her and took her hand. "I know you said that night in London a commitment is the last thing you're looking for, but I'm really hoping you're going to make an exception for me."

She wanted him to put that ring on her finger so badly her whole body shook.

"Marry me," he rasped. "Marry me so I don't have to feel as awful as I've felt the past few weeks without you."

Her whole body went numb. She was trying to find her voice when a groan sounded behind her.

"Come on, Izzie, just say yes."

She turned around to find that the entire Warriors team had assembled beside the reporters, helmets in hand.

"I don't know," she managed to tease. "I was thinking of making him suffer." She turned back to Alex, so ridiculously hot on one knee, she knew this moment would be imprinted on her mind forever. "I guess my dream one-night stand really backfired on me, huh?"

"That depends on how you define 'backfire.'" The sexy glint in his eyes made her hot all over. "If that means a million more of those before we grow old and tired, I'm okay with it."

Nick coughed. "Still filming." Izzie shoved her hand forward. Alex slid the ring on her finger, steadying her shaking hands with his own. The outrageously beautiful ring sparkled like pink fire in the glare of the stadium lights.

It fit perfectly.

The team whooped and hollered their approval. Alex got to his feet and pulled her into his arms for a kiss that was apparently not fit for broadcast because she heard Nick call it a wrap and fade into the background. Izzie sighed and wrapped her arms around Alex's neck. Because never in a million years would she have thought she'd get her quarterback.

When Alex finally set her away from him with reluctant hands he had a scowl on his face. "The only problem with this grand plan of mine is I can't kiss you like I want to."

"Patience," she murmured. "How many celebratory drinks do you think will do it?"

"One," he said flatly. "I'm buying them one and we're done."

He tucked her into his side as they walked toward the players. Her heart was so full she thought it might burst. "We've just left one question unanswered," she mused.

He lifted a brow. "What?"

"Damion."

"Damion? Who's Damion?"

"The hero from my book," she reminded him. "You asked me if he was good in bed…"

He shot her an amused look. "*Now* you're going to tell me? What's the verdict?"

"You are way, *way* better."

His shout of laughter rang out. Pulling to a halt, he lifted her up on tiptoes and captured her mouth in another of those long, sweet kisses that promised forever. "Give me an hour to celebrate with the team," he said huskily, "and I promise to blow that out of the water."

* * * * *

Mills & Boon® Hardback

September 2014

ROMANCE

The Housekeeper's Awakening	Sharon Kendrick
More Precious than a Crown	Carol Marinelli
Captured by the Sheikh	Kate Hewitt
A Night in the Prince's Bed	Chantelle Shaw
Damaso Claims His Heir	Annie West
Changing Constantinou's Game	Jennifer Hayward
The Ultimate Revenge	Victoria Parker
Tycoon's Temptation	Trish Morey
The Party Dare	Anne Oliver
Sleeping with the Soldier	Charlotte Phillips
All's Fair in Lust & War	Amber Page
Dressed to Thrill	Bella Frances
Interview with a Tycoon	Cara Colter
Her Boss by Arrangement	Teresa Carpenter
In Her Rival's Arms	Alison Roberts
Frozen Heart, Melting Kiss	Ellie Darkins
After One Forbidden Night...	Amber McKenzie
Dr Perfect on Her Doorstep	Lucy Clark

MEDICAL

A Secret Shared...	Marion Lennox
Flirting with the Doc of Her Dreams	Janice Lynn
The Doctor Who Made Her Love Again	Susan Carlisle
The Maverick Who Ruled Her Heart	Susan Carlisle

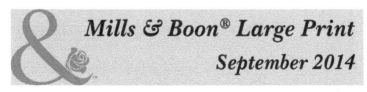

Mills & Boon® Large Print
September 2014

ROMANCE

The Only Woman to Defy Him	Carol Marinelli
Secrets of a Ruthless Tycoon	Cathy Williams
Gambling with the Crown	Lynn Raye Harris
The Forbidden Touch of Sanguardo	Julia James
One Night to Risk it All	Maisey Yates
A Clash with Cannavaro	Elizabeth Power
The Truth About De Campo	Jennifer Hayward
Expecting the Prince's Baby	Rebecca Winters
The Millionaire's Homecoming	Cara Colter
The Heir of the Castle	Scarlet Wilson
Twelve Hours of Temptation	Shoma Narayanan

HISTORICAL

Unwed and Unrepentant	Marguerite Kaye
Return of the Prodigal Gilvry	Ann Lethbridge
A Traitor's Touch	Helen Dickson
Yield to the Highlander	Terri Brisbin
Return of the Viking Warrior	Michelle Styles

MEDICAL

Waves of Temptation	Marion Lennox
Risk of a Lifetime	Caroline Anderson
To Play with Fire	Tina Beckett
The Dangers of Dating Dr Carvalho	Tina Beckett
Uncovering Her Secrets	Amalie Berlin
Unlocking the Doctor's Heart	Susanne Hampton

0814 GEN STD LP

Mills & Boon® Hardback
October 2014

ROMANCE

MEDICAL

Mills & Boon® Large Print

October 2014

ROMANCE

Ravelli's Defiant Bride	Lynne Graham
When Da Silva Breaks the Rules	Abby Green
The Heartbreaker Prince	Kim Lawrence
The Man She Can't Forget	Maggie Cox
A Question of Honour	Kate Walker
What the Greek Can't Resist	Maya Blake
An Heir to Bind Them	Dani Collins
Becoming the Prince's Wife	Rebecca Winters
Nine Months to Change His Life	Marion Lennox
Taming Her Italian Boss	Fiona Harper
Summer with the Millionaire	Jessica Gilmore

HISTORICAL

Scars of Betrayal	Sophia James
Scandal's Virgin	Louise Allen
An Ideal Companion	Anne Ashley
Surrender to the Viking	Joanna Fulford
No Place for an Angel	Gail Whitiker

MEDICAL

200 Harley Street: Surgeon in a Tux	Carol Marinelli
200 Harley Street: Girl from the Red Carpet	Scarlet Wilson
Flirting with the Socialite Doc	Melanie Milburne
His Diamond Like No Other	Lucy Clark
The Last Temptation of Dr Dalton	Robin Gianna
Resisting Her Rebel Hero	Lucy Ryder

MILLS & BOON®

Why shop at millsandboon.co.uk?

Each year, thousands of romance readers find their
perfect read at millsandboon.co.uk. That's because
we're passionate about bringing you the very best
romantic fiction. Here are some of the advantages
of shopping at www.millsandboon.co.uk:

* **Get new books first**—you'll be able to buy your
  favourite books one month before they hit
  the shops

* **Get exclusive discounts**—you'll also be able to buy
  our specially created monthly collections, with up
  to 50% off the RRP

* **Find your favourite authors**—latest news,
  interviews and new releases for all your favourite
  authors and series on our website, plus ideas for
  what to try next

* **Join in**—once you've bought your favourite books,
  don't forget to register with us to rate, review and
  join in the discussions

Visit **www.millsandboon.co.uk**
for all this and more today!

MILLS_WEB_HB